The Road Home

Susannah Hayden

A sequel to *Farther Along the Road*

Heartsong Presents

A note from the Author:
I love to hear from my readers! You may write to me at the
following address:

Susannah Hayden
Author Relations
P.O. Box 719
Uhrichsville, OH 44683

ISBN 1-55748-748-0

THE ROAD HOME

Cover illustration by Kay Salem.

PRINTED IN THE U.S.A.

Julie Covington knows that her art is more than just hard work...but what?

"I wish I could have known your grandmother. The woman in *Triumph* is a woman of faith."

"Do you really think so?" Julie looked directly at Charles for the first time in this conversation.

"That's the way you painted her. And you paint only what you see. You've said that yourself. I have to believe she knew God."

"She did." Julie hugged a pillow under her good arm. "There's so much about God that I don't understand," she said quietly.

"Who can understand God? If we could understand, we would not need Him." Charles leaned forward in his chair and rested his elbows on his knees. "Julie, don't let your lack of knowledge get in the way of expressing your faith."

"How can I believe things that I don't understand?"

"You paint things you don't understand all the time."

"What do you mean?"

"Look at Aunt Joanna's eyes. Did you consciously sit down and analyze why her eyes are so bright? Were your strokes on the paper an act of understanding? . . .And think of *Triumph*. Did you analyze all those images of your grandmother or did you just paint what you knew to be true?"

Julie nodded slowly. She was beginning to understand . . . . "You're saying that I can believe more than I understand?"

"Absolutely."

SUSANNAH HAYDEN is the pen name of a versatile and gifted author of fiction and biography for both adults and children. Susannah makes her home in Illinois with her husband and children.

Books by Susannah Hayden

HEARTSONG PRESENTS
HP14—A Matter of Choice
HP69—Between Love and Loyalty
HP77—The Road Before Me
HP113—Between the Memory and the Moment
HP117—Farther Along the Road

ROMANCE READER—TWO BOOKS IN ONE
RR9—Summer's Wind Blowing & Spring Waters Rushing

Don't miss out on any of our super romances. Write to us at the following address for information on our newest releases and club information.

Heartsong Presents Readers' Service
P.O. Box 719
Uhrichsville, OH 44683

one

"Julie? Are you awake?" Della Paxton asked.

"Yes, Della. I'm up." Julie Covington, still snuggled in her robe, pulled the comb through her tangled wet hair. "I'll be down in a few minutes."

It was a morning ritual that had been going on for more than a year. Della would climb the stairs to the third floor and call for Julie, who was always awake before she got there.

"It makes me nervous to have you up there on the third floor by yourself," Della had said more than once.

"I like the room and I don't mind the isolation," Julie always replied.

"Take your time," Della said now. "If you want to sleep in—"

"No, I'll be there," Julie assured her friend through the closed door.

This, too, was an ongoing playful argument between the two of them. Julie had moved into Leed House shortly after the bed and breakfast inn had opened. At first it was supposed to be a short stay, for which she expected to pay the usual rates. But Della had soon pressured her into staying indefinitely and promised her the privacy of the tower room on the third floor. Julie still wanted to pay, but Della would not accept her money. Finally, they had compromised on the idea that Julie would work part-time around the inn to earn her keep. One of her main duties was helping with breakfast.

Julie was not new to Leed House. Before moving in, she had visited twice before. The first time had been more than two years ago, when she had spent a summer in Seabridge, Maine. She had discovered that her grandmother's long-neglected childhood home, Leed House, was undergoing renovation by new owners and would emerge as a shiny, new bed and breakfast inn. When Della Paxton discovered Julie's connection with the old house, she had quickly taken Julie under her wing. Although Julie did not stay at Leed House during that visit, she enjoyed free run of the property. She had spent that summer sketching and painting the inn from every possible angle. The largest of her series of images of the house hung in the parlor for all the guests to enjoy. Della loved to make sure the visitors knew that the artist lived in the house.

A few months later, Julie returned briefly to Leed House during a break from her senior year of college. This time she made two significant connections that drew her back once again after graduation. First, she met David Flagg, the owner of a prestigious art gallery in Seabridge. The undistinguished, typical small coastal town seemed an unlikely place for such a successful art business; nevertheless, the Flagg Gallery thrived. Its reputation flourished throughout New England and into New York City. David was enthusiastic about Julie's work and willing to take a risk on an unknown artist. He had been successful at selling several of Julie's paintings and wanted her to supply more.

Julie's introduction to David had been arranged by the other significant connection of that first visit: Larry Paxton, Della's son. During Julie's first summer in Seabridge, while she was still in college, Larry had seemed friendly, but distant. She had quietly wrestled with confusing feelings about him. She hardly knew him, yet she found herself watching for his movements around the house. It was clear, however, that Larry, who was already in his late twenties, saw her as barely more than an adolescent. Having left the rat race of the accounting world in New York City, he was content to help his mother refurbish the old house.

Gradually their relationship had changed, starting when Larry visited her in Illinois while on a business trip. After that, when Julie had come to Seabridge to stay, Larry had been the first one to show his delight. In fact, he had urged her to come. Now, fifteen months later, they had an easygoing, affectionate relationship that they both enjoyed. Larry believed that Julie was an artist, sometimes more than she believed it herself.

Julie laid the comb aside and sighed with satisfaction. Life had certainly been comfortable since she had come to Seabridge.

"Ah, Grammy, you would have liked what they've done with Leed House," she said aloud as she gazed at a photo on her dresser.

Julie's grandmother, Julienne Leed Covington, had grown up in this very room, many decades earlier. It was in this room that a seventeen-year-old girl had confessed to her diary that she was in love with Lorenzo Scorzo, the mysterious, dark Italian man of whom her parents disapproved. Lorenzo had been sent away and Julienne never knew what had become of him. Instead, she had gone on to marry Colin Covington, the grandfather whom Julie had never known. Two years ago, when Larry was tearing out a wall, Julie had found the diary and learned the secrets of her grandmother's youth.

For months Julie had been fascinated by what might have been, had events been different more than seventy years ago. Her grandmother's story had been complicated when Julie discovered that Lorenzo Scorzo was Della's father and Larry's grandfather.

As Julie's relationship with Larry evolved, her fascination with the past deepened. Two generations after Julienne and

Lorenzo were denied love, their grandchildren were gradually discovering it. Were they replaying the past and taking the story to a new ending?

Julie stood before the dresser and fingered the silver frame that held the old photograph of her grandmother as a sixteen-year-old girl, not yet knowing that her womanhood was just around the corner. Grammy had succumbed to Alzheimer's disease and lived her last years unaware of past or present. She had died the previous winter, her mind at last released from its cage. Julie, her namesake, had inherited most of her personal memorabilia. This particular photo was a favorite and she kept it near her all the time. As she studied it periodically, she could almost feel the presence of the girl who had lived in this room all those years ago.

Before her grandmother died, Julie had done sketch after sketch of the old woman, with her proud bearing, her piercing but vacant eyes, the strong jaw line. Julie had prepared for months for the portrait she eventually painted, a painting she thought was her best work ever and something she would never part with, no matter what the price.

Julie moved to the overstuffed chair that she kept in front of the window. Resting her face in her hands and propping her elbows on the window ledge, she looked out over the front lawn of Leed House. The grass was a fleeting shade of green, as if tomorrow it might be brown. The cluster of maple and oak trees, which her ancestor Captain Mason Leed had planted, stood proudly against the sky, their branches heavy with variegated leaves awaiting nature's cue that it was time for them to drop. The morning air was chilly, but Julie had swung open the hinged glass windows as she did every morning and looked out without the interference of a screen or shutter.

The view from the tower room on the third floor of Leed

House was unsurpassable, in Julie's opinion. From this vantage point she could see the sprawling neighborhood with its 200-year-old houses and spacious lawns. Children, with no concept of the history of the homes they lived in, dotted the neighborhood waiting for school buses. Life rolled forward and, with each advancing frame, the past grew more distant. Those children lived in a world dominated by the here and now, weighty backpacks, and last-minute goodbye kisses. What did they know of the founders of their town or the families that had lived in their homes a hundred years ago?

Julie watched as a leaf finally surrendered to the downward pull and detached itself from a trembling twig. Swaying back and forth, it floated to the ground and fell softly onto the pile of leaves that had fallen the day before. Instinctively, Julie reached for her sketch pad and began drawing the single leaf gently making its way to the ground. She perched herself on the arm of an overstuffed chair and used the wide window ledge as a makeshift table. Deftly she captured the swaying with circular strokes of her pencil. These were motions she had been going through for months. She never grew tired of the morning survey of the neighborhood. The major elements did not change: the houses, the roads, the trees, the telephone poles. But there was always something new to look at—like today's solitary falling leaf or yesterday's scurrying chipmunk, or the multi-shaded gray sky before last week's thunderstorm.

Reluctantly Julie set the sketch book aside and invaded her closet in search of something to wear. She dressed comfortably in jeans and a loose sweater, knowing that the day would be long and busy. In fact, the next several days were likely to go by in a whirlwind. David Flagg was featuring the work of Julie Covington at a showing in his gallery that weekend. Julie kept expecting that David would change his mind and say he had made a mistake, but so far he had not. His efforts at the gallery these days were aimed in her direction.

Julie took a last glance in the mirror, smoothed a stray blond hair, and headed downstairs. She resisted the impulse to slide down the polished banister and land at the bottom of the stairs, two floors down. After all, there were paying guests in the inn and they expected a measure of decorum from the staff.

Popping her head in the kitchen, she said, "Good morning, Della."

"Well, there you are. Glad to see you really are up. Sometimes I wonder, you know. You get to daydreaming or something and I'm not sure you're coming down."

Julie went to the cupboard for breakfast dishes. "I always make it down before the guests; that's the important thing."

"I do have to give you credit for that." Della filled a basket with warm cinnamon rolls. "You don't have to come down at all, you know. I can manage breakfast alone. And I would save something for you to eat, so don't use that excuse."

"I have a better idea," Julie said. "Why don't you sleep in some morning and let me handle breakfast?"

Della set her jaw. "Don't be ridiculous. This is my inn. I will serve breakfast."

Julie laughed and gave up. "Well, as long as I'm here, I might as well help." She picked up her stack of antique china plates and went into the smaller of two dining rooms. There would be five guests, plus Larry. Della never sat down to eat, and Julie usually kept Della company in the kitchen, refilling serving dishes as needed.

The back door off the kitchen creaked open and a moment later Julie heard Larry's voice murmuring in the kitchen. Then he came through the door.

"Good morning," he said.

She smiled warmly at him. "Good morning."

"I have something for you." He held out an envelope

toward her.

"Oh?" She examined the envelope. "A telegram? Do people still send telegrams?"

"Apparently someone does. You just got one."

Curious, she ripped off the end of the envelope and scanned the message. Her shoulders sagged immediately.

"Bad news?" Larry asked.

Julie nodded and began reading. "Change in plans. Dad threw his back out yesterday. Confined to bed. Cannot come to opening of show. Wish you success and many sales. All our love. Mom and Dad." She stared at the yellow paper, hardly believing what it said.

"Julie, I'm sorry. I know you were looking forward to having your parents here for the show."

She stuffed the page back into the envelope and stuck it in her back pocket. "Oh, well, as they say, the show must go on."

"We'll send them lots of photos." Larry stood behind her and rubbed her shoulder sympathetically. In the background, a kitchen timer chimed.

"I'd better get this table set. It's almost eight o'clock. Then I guess I'll call home and see how Dad is."

Larry stopped the nervous motion of her hands and took the stack of plates. "You go call now. I'll do this."

two

"No, Mom, don't worry about it," Julie said into the telephone in the hall. "Dad can't possibly travel and he needs you there with him right now."

"I just hate to miss your first show," Liz Covington lamented.

Julie laughed. "My 'first' show. That means you think there will be others."

"Certainly there will be. And I'll be there the next time."

"Thanks, Mom, for the vote of confidence. Give my love to Dad." She hung up the phone, feeling consoled slightly.

"Everything all right?" Larry said, popping his head out of the kitchen.

"Dad is probably as disappointed as I am," Julie said. "He was looking forward to finally getting to see Leed House on this trip."

"They should still come, as soon as he's better."

"Perhaps," Julie nodded. "Actually it's better this way. If the show is a disaster, I won't have to be embarrassed in front of my parents."

"There you go again, berating yourself for no good reason."

"Sorry," she mumbled. "An old habit."

Della's voice came authoritatively from the kitchen. "Larry, ring the bell."

"Yes, ma'am."

In one of her forays into a steady stream of flea markets, Della had uncovered an old bell off the front of a ship and

12

had immediately adopted it for Leed House. It rang every morning promptly at eight o'clock. Today, like every day, Larry gave it one firm stroke and the gong resounded throughout the house.

Larry took his place at the head of the table to play host and Julie went into the kitchen to help carry serving dishes. Warm cinnamon rolls, scrambled eggs, hash browns, and bacon constituted the day's breakfast menu.

"Oh, good, cinnamon rolls again!" The exclamation came from Mary Ellen Ventura as she slid heavily into her usual chair. Mary Ellen had been at Leed House for over a week and had developed several habits, especially involving eating. Thirtyish and stout, Mary Ellen was from Iowa and had saved for years for a trip to New England to see the fall colors. Bemoaning the fact that she was in Maine alone rather than on the honeymoon of her dreams, she nevertheless packed her days with the activities she had envisioned for several years. Today, dressed in a denim skirt, a sweater, and thick socks and hiking boots, she was serious about exploring the county and collecting specimens of dried leaves to take home for her scrapbook.

"Are you enjoying the fall colors?" Julie asked pleasantly, as she had several times before. She set a pitcher of orange juice in front of Mary Ellen, knowing she would want it momentarily.

"Yes, they are just marvelous!" exuded Mary Ellen. "I could walk for miles and miles and not get tired of looking at them. I never realized there were so many shades of red."

"Don't the leaves turn colors in Iowa?" Larry asked.

"Oh, not like this! Nothing like this!" was Mary Ellen's quick reply. "There's absolutely no comparison."

"Coffee?" Julie offered. Mary Ellen held up her cup.

"Even the coffee seems better here," Mary Ellen said. "I

don't think I ever want to go home."

"Do what they're doing," Larry said, gesturing to the young couple who had just entered the room. "Sell everything you own and live off a boat."

Theo Butler laughed and shook his finger at Larry. The two men, about the same age, had struck up a rapport in only a couple of days.

"Don't knock it until you've tried it," Theo said.

"It's not so different than what you did," his wife, Lisa, said. "You left New York City to live in a small, quiet New England town. We just picked a boat instead of a two-hundred-year-old inn."

"Why are you here?" Mary Ellen asked.

"To see New England, of course," Lisa replied.

"No, I mean here at the inn. If you are living off a boat, what are you doing here?"

Theo looked at his wife and smiled slyly. "Lisa wanted to see if she still had her land legs."

Lisa slapped him with her cloth napkin. "I just wanted to be closer to the shops for a couple of days. Seabridge has some of the best shops around and Christmas is coming."

"Christmas!" A deep male voice boomed from the other end of the room. "I can't believe my ears. Someone is thinking about Christmas in the middle of October?" Dayton Edwards never entered a room without drawing attention to himself. He sat down across from Mary Ellen and quickly entered the conversation.

"That would be Lisa," Theo said. "She's never caught without a plan."

"My plan for Christmas is not to have a plan," Dayton said. "It's more exciting that way." He reached for a cinnamon roll. "Pass the eggs, please. Besides, I've found that not giving presents cuts down substantially on my end-of-year expenses."

Julie watched Dayton Edwards for a moment. He was in his early thirties, boyishly handsome, curly dark hair, eyes that smiled all the time. He had been at Leed House for four or five days now and had not revealed his intended departure date or his reason for being in Seabridge. But he seemed pleasant and Julie actually enjoyed his bantering. He reminded her of her brother, Ted, who could always be depended on to keep the conversation rolling.

Julie looked up just in time to see the final guest arrive. Fenway Lamp was an older, heavyset businessman who had been to the inn several times before while passing through Seabridge. Julie was not quite sure what his business was. Mr. Lamp was not one to talk much; he just enjoyed the privacy and quietude of the inn and the convenience of being close to town. Julie would have been surprised if he had entered into the breakfast time banter and, true to her expectations, he did not.

"What's everybody up to today?" Larry asked. "Does anyone need help arranging something?"

"I'm hiking north today," Mary Ellen said. "I discovered a new trail at the edge of town."

Theo looked at his wife. "I have a feeling we're going shopping."

"How about you, Mr. Lamp?" Larry said. "Can I help you with anything?"

"That won't be necessary, Mr. Paxton. I should be concluding my business fairly soon."

"Well, Dayton," Larry said, pouring himself more coffee. "That leaves you."

"Don't worry, I won't be in your hair today." Dayton grinned at his host. "I've got places to go, people to see, and so forth."

Della whizzed into the room with a fresh platter of hash

browns. "More potatoes for anyone?"

Dayton nodded his head. "Thanks. I'm a growing boy." He helped himself to a generous second portion. "How about you, Julie? What will you fill your day with?"

Julie had been straightening dishes on the sideboard and had not expected to be addressed.

"Me? The usual, I guess."

"Painting?"

She nodded, offering no further information.

"She's being too modest," Della interjected. "She has a show starting the day after tomorrow. I hope you all can come."

"A show!" Mary Ellen exclaimed. "You mean your paintings will be for sale?"

"Some of them," Julie answered.

"Have you done any of the fall colors?" Mary Ellen asked exactly the question Julie expected.

"Actually, I have," Julie said. "A couple of small ones from last year."

"I must come and see! Wouldn't that be the perfect souvenir?"

"I know I'll be there," Dayton said. "I saw a flyer in a shop window yesterday. It sounds like a delightful way to spend an evening. And of course, since I know the lovely artist, I couldn't possibly consider leaving Seabridge until after the show." Dayton caught Julie's eye, but she quickly looked away. While Dayton was more than likeable, Julie felt awkward with his attention.

"Here, let me take your plates," she said. Uncomfortable in the limelight, Julie wanted to turn the attention to more mundane matters. She began stacking used plates expertly on one arm and soon disappeared into the kitchen. Della was not far behind her.

"You know, you shouldn't do that," Della said.

"Do what?"

"Change the subject every time someone has something nice to say about you."

"Do I do that?" Julie turned on the water in the sink and began rinsing plates.

"Every time."

"That's just me, I guess."

"That's just you not believing in yourself, you mean."

Julie could tell that Della was moving into one of her high-speak talkative moods.

"You could sell a lot of paintings, you know, if you would just let people pay a little attention to you. I know, you're going to say that the paintings speak for themselves, and I suppose that's true enough, but it certainly couldn't hurt anything to be proud of your work and let people know about it. I try to tell as many people as I can about you, and I send them right down to the Flagg Gallery. I know for a fact that two of my friends have bought your paintings—"

"Mom."

Della wheeled around to see Larry standing in the doorway. "What is it, Larry?"

"You're doing it again."

"Am I?" She knew what he was talking about—her inclination to take over a room and say everything on her mind in one long speech.

"Yes, you are."

"Then I'll stop. I've got to go into town for some groceries. I'll just get ready to do that." Abruptly but good-naturedly she left the kitchen.

"I don't believe it," Julie said, smiling but shaking her head. "She took off without giving me her usual lecture about how I should let her clean up the breakfast dishes so that I could go be an artist."

"It is a bit strange," Larry agreed.

"What is she conniving?"

Larry laughed. "Maybe she just needs some groceries, like she said."

Julie cocked her head to one side and looked at Larry. "And if you believe that, then I've got some land for you in Florida," she said. "In any event, she has left me in peace to do my work." She turned back to the sink. "What are you up to today?"

"I've got to pay bills. It costs a lot to keep this place running, you know. It's my job to juggle things and keep the creditors happy."

"It's good practice. We wouldn't want you to forget how to be an accountant."

"Now you sound like my mother."

"I'm flattered. Your mother is a wonderful person." Julie headed back to the dining room with a tray to gather up more dishes. The guests had dispersed. Larry trailed after her.

"You know what I mean," he said.

"Maybe I do, maybe I don't." Julie piled the tray with dishes. She had become quite adept at balancing a heavy tray.

"Okay, I concede that my mother is a wonderful person." Back in the kitchen, Larry took the tray from Julie and set it beside the sink. "But I'm more interested in another wonderful person." He caught her hand and tugged on her fingers. "Let's go out tonight."

"Where?"

"Anywhere. You choose. We'll have dinner. You need to relax. You're so wound up lately."

"I know. I'm nervous about the show." She tried to pull away from him, but Larry would not let go of her hand.

"David Flagg has everything under control. I just spoke with him yesterday. Everything's fine."

"I know," Julie said, finally giving in and no longer resisting Larry's attention. "I can't help myself. I just need to keep moving."

"I'll make you a deal. You can be nervous all you want during the day, but when dinner time comes, you relax and let me pamper you."

She smiled. "I guess that sounds fair. Besides, it'll give your mother a break. None of the guests plan to be here for dinner either."

"Then we have a plan."

"I suppose so."

Larry leaned forward and kissed her cheek. "I'll see you about six o'clock, then. I'll be in my study most of the day if you need me for anything."

"I'll be at the gallery," she said softly as she watched him leave the room.

Julie turned back to the dirty dishes. They were too delicate for the dishwasher, so she would have to wash them by hand. But she did not mind just as long as she had something to keep her busy.

Cleaning up did not take long. She was giving the counter one last swipe with the dishrag when Dayton Edwards poked his head in from the dining room.

"Hi," he said simply.

"Hi," Julie responded, surprised to see him. "Can I do something for you? Don't tell me you're hungry again already."

He laughed gently. "Nothing like that." He came into the room and leaned against the counter she had just wiped, standing close to her. "I just wanted to offer my sincere congratulations on your show. It's quite an achievement, isn't it?"

"Well, it's not New York City, and it's only for a weekend." Julie stepped back from Dayton and hung the dishrag over the faucet.

"Still, it's important," Dayton insisted. "A first step. I just want you to know I'm happy for you."

"Well, thank you." Julie barely knew Dayton Edwards. Why should he be offering personal congratulations for her achievement? If Dayton was mindful of her awkward feeling, he did not show it.

"The next couple of days are not too busy for me, so if you need anything, I'll be happy to help out."

"Thanks, but I think David Flagg has taken care of all the arrangements."

"Great." He smiled deeply into her eyes, too deeply, and locked her gaze. "I look forward to being one of the first to view your collection." Then he left.

Julie was not sure of the real reason he had stopped in the kitchen. There was a lot about Dayton of which she was unsure.

three

The drive to the Flagg Gallery was only a few minutes long. While she made the familiar turns, Julie tried to focus her thoughts. The opening of the show was only two days away. David Flagg had his part of the preparation under control. He had done so many shows before that he simply worked off a checklist based on his experience. In his mind, there was no such thing as being caught off guard.

Julie, on the other hand, was swamped with last-minute details. Some of her paintings were untitled and she was adamant that she wanted a title on everything by the time of the show. And Della had talked her into getting her shoulder-length blond hair trimmed softly around her face before the show, so she had to do that today. And her dress was ready to be picked up.

Her first stop would be the gallery. She parked down the block, got out and locked the car, and started up the sidewalk. Her mind was spinning so fast she hardly noticed anyone else was around.

"Well, hello there," came a voice.

She looked up and saw Charles Brooke walking toward her. Involuntarily she looked the other way for a fraction of a second, but she knew she could not avoid this encounter.

Charles Brooke was not unpleasant. In fact, he was very pleasant and Julie enjoyed his engaging sense of humor. His British sounding name and his position as pastor of the hundred-year-old community church made Julie expect something very different than what Charles was. He constantly surprised her with his comfortable personality and often walked around town in jeans, shirt, and loafers instead of the black suit she expected a clergyman to wear. No, the problem was not Charles Brooke. The problem was what he wanted her to do.

"If I didn't know better, I'd say you've been avoiding me," Charles said, smiling good-naturedly.

She looked sheepish. "Well. . .not exactly."

"You've been busy with the show, I suppose."

"Yes, actually, very busy." It was an honest defense.

"Well, your hands may be busy all the time, but I hope your mind has had a chance to think about what we discussed."

Reluctantly, Julie said, "I do have some ideas. I even made some sketches. But I'm not sure they are what you want."

"You're the artist," Charles said. "I want you to do a painting for the church foyer, but I want it to be really yours. I hope you don't feel as if I'm trying to dictate to you about what to paint."

"No, that's not it."

"Then what is it, Julie? I want the painting to be as pleasurable for you to paint as it is for the church to receive."

"I guess I'm just not sure I can do an authentic painting that communicates anything about faith. I've had so many doubts the last couple of years." She thought of the illness of her grandmother and the surrounding family squabbles, a romantic relationship that had broken off abruptly during her senior year of college because she was unable to make a commitment, and, finally, her grandmother's death. She shrugged her shoulders. "I haven't been much of a model of faith. It's hard to paint something I don't feel."

Charles was silent.

Julie hastened to add, "Don't get me wrong. I do believe in Jesus, and when I come to church I am able to worship sincerely. But beyond that, it's such a struggle. I have so many questions. How can I inspire other people about something I'm not very good at?"

"Faith is not something people are good at in general."

"Other people seem so much better at it than I am. I'm so unsure."

"Are you really so unsure?" Charles asked quietly.

Julie squinted at him in the fall sunlight, taken aback by his question. She probed his eyes for more explanation.

"When I look at your paintings, Julie, I see a light shining out of them. It may be in only one corner, or it may be obscured by haze, but it's there. In every painting. Whether you were intentional about it or not."

"Larry once said the same thing."

"I assure you, this is not a conspiracy. This light is really there."

"I have always been fascinated by light," she conceded. "But what does that have to do with anything?"

"Why are you fascinated by light? Why do you see light dancing in the darkest places?"

"I just paint what I see."

"You do much more than that."

"No, I don't."

"Then I think you see more than you give yourself credit for." Charles looked at his watch. "I'm late for a meeting, and I'm sure you've got somewhere you're supposed to be. Bring the sketches by, Julie. I'd like to see them."

"Okay, I will," she promised feebly, not sure she wanted to commit herself even to that small step.

Charles strode off down the sidewalk to his meeting. Julie proceeded at a much slower pace toward the gallery. Charles always mystified her. Every encounter with him left her wondering what he was really after. Why was it so important to him that she paint something for the foyer? Maybe her work would not even fit in well with the historic atmosphere of the building. There were other worthy artists in the area. Why had he chosen her? And why was he so persistent?

Julie had started going to the little community church only out of curiosity. It was the same small church that her grandmother's family had attended in the early part of the century: the same stone building, the same solid oak, handcrafted pews. There were other churches in town, bigger ones, more progressive ones. But Julie liked the idea that she could sit where her grandmother once sat. It was for this reason that she chose the community church. Especially after her grandmother died, Julie found solace in going to that place. Her intentions had not been the best at first. She knew she ought to have a better reason for going to church. Nevertheless, she had begun attending regularly. Della and Larry went frequently as well, so it was easy to find herself more involved than she had intended to be. She had even helped to make a quilt that was sent overseas to a refugee camp.

Charles was steadily present through all of this. He understood her fascination with her grandmother's childhood and indulged her by letting her see the handwritten church records of that era. There, in black ink and an elaborate script, was her grandmother's name, date of birth, and date of baptism. At one point Julie had almost stopped going, because she felt that her reasons were not very good ones for going to church. But Charles had not given up on her. Whatever her reasons, he welcomed her and challenged her. Now she faced the biggest challenge ever: Could she paint a portrayal of faith for the foyer?

She reached the gallery's front door and shrugged off her ponderings. She had more immediate concerns; her dilemma with Charles would have to wait. She pushed the door open and went in.

"Good morning, David," she said to the man behind the counter. The fiftyish man with gray hair barely looked up as she entered.

"Good morning. I need that list of titles today, Julie." As usual, David Flagg greeted her with complete professionalism. He seldom had anything but business on his mind. "If I don't get them by noon, I'll have to hang the paintings with tags that say 'Untitled.'" Now he looked up at her, clearly looking for a response.

"You'll have them by noon, I promise. There are just a few that I'm still tinkering with."

"Why don't you let me have what you already decided on, and I can get the calligrapher started on them."

"Sure. I'll get the list." Julie walked the length of the shop to a small desk in the back and fished a sheet of paper out of a pile. David had followed her back. "Here," she said, handing him the sheet of paper. "These I'm sure of. These four I'm still thinking about."

"I'm nearly ready for the portrait of your grandmother," David said, moving on to the next item on his list. "It's still here, isn't it?"

"Yes, in the back room. The large canvas next to the door."

"Let's have a look at it right now. I think I've found a frame for it at last."

Julie's eyes lit up. "Great! Can I see it this afternoon?"

"Anytime after two o'clock. It should be back from the refinisher by then."

Julie led the way to the back room where the oversized painting sat on two easels. David flipped on the light.

Her grandmother's image gazed back at Julie. In the center of the canvas, the focal point, was an image that seemed timeless. Was the woman young or was she old? It was difficult to tell. Julie was pleased that she had achieved this effect.

Circling the main image were shadowy profiles; one blended into the other, the mood of the painting shifting subtly as the viewer scanned the circle. When examined carefully, the changing images revealed a progression of ages. The overall effect was one of endurance, triumph, and pride of a lifetime. Julie called the painting simply, *Triumph.*

"This is a very nice piece of work, Julie," David said. "I'm sure I could get a good price for it."

"It's not for sale," Julie said adamantly. "Put that in big letters on the tag. Not for sale."

"Obviously you've made up your mind about this one."

"Selling this painting would be like giving away my grandmother. I can't do that."

"I understand. We'll take good care of it."

"Thanks, David. Thanks for everything. I still can't believe this is happening."

"Never mind that." David waved away her sentimentality. "We both have a lot to gain from this show. Let's just get the job done well."

He stuffed her list of titles into his shirt pocket and headed toward the front of the store. "Vanessa should be in soon. Can you mind the shop for a few minutes while I look after this?"

"Sure, no problem."

Julie took her remaining list of titles and a freshly sharpened pencil and wandered up front. It was not unusual for David to ask her to look after things for a few minutes. She had even sold a couple of paintings to tourists. But she hoped Vanessa would not be too much longer.

Julie admired Vanessa, perhaps because they were so different. Vanessa Parker was a few years older than Julie and excelled at everything she did. She dressed impeccably, prepared gourmet meals as if they were ordinary events, made friends with everyone in town, and did her job with astonishing success. While David concentrated on selling art to collectors or individuals, Vanessa pursued upscale, successful businesses and persuaded them to hang art in their offices. She had come to the Flagg Gallery, uninvited, three years earlier and sold David on the idea of adding a line of office art to his enterprise. Business had boomed since then. They had initiated a subscription program in which clients would rent art and get three fresh pieces every six months. Many of the rental pieces eventually sold. Vanessa's success was part of the reason David Flagg could afford to take chances on unknown artists like Julie Covington. She traveled around the entire state drumming up business. It seemed that no one could resist her. She had placed four of Julie's paintings in the last two years.

At first Julie had been awed by Vanessa and found herself tongue-tied in her presence. But she warmed up to the saleswoman, as everyone did, and they had become close friends. At least twice a month they ate dinner together and indulged in long intimate conversations. Vanessa was the only one to whom Julie confided every feeling she had about Larry as their relationship developed.

The bell jangled as the front door swung open. Julie looked up expectantly.

"Oh, good, you're here," she said, seeing Vanessa.

"Hi ya, Julie!" Vanessa said with her usual exuberance. With a heave she set her over-the-shoulder bag on the counter. Her gray lightweight wool suit was unrumpled. She looked like she had just stepped out of a fashion catalog. "Are you about ready for the big day?"

"I think so. I'm supposed to get my hair cut today." Julie nervously twisted a wad of hair around her fingers.

"What about your dress?"

"I found one, basic black, but it had to be altered. It should be ready this afternoon."

"Shoes?"

"Yep."

"Stylish but comfortable?"

"Just like you said."

"Accessories?"

"My grandmother's pearl necklace and matching earrings."

"Nice choice. Sounds like you're all set." Vanessa scanned the shop. "Where's David?"

"He took the titles to the calligrapher. Then he'll be in the showroom most of the day."

"Good. That'll give me an excuse to stay in the shop and relax a little bit, instead of running around the highways."

"How did the last sales trip go?"

"Great. Sold one more of yours, as a matter of fact. They want it right after the show."

"Wow. You're incredible, Vanni. How did David ever get along without you?"

"He should be wondering that himself," Vanni quipped. "I'm making him a rich man." She gave Julie a puzzled expression. "What are you doing here anyway? You should be off getting pampered."

"There's plenty of time for that. I still have to decide about some titles. I promised David I'd have them by noon."

"I'll mind the store now, so you can go back to your corner and work on them. Shoo!"

Julie laughed and followed Vanni's instructions. In an attempt to settle down and at least appear organized, Julie straightened a stack of papers on the desk and dropped a used paper cup into the trash can. When the bell jangled, she could not keep herself from looking up. From her vantage point in the back of the store, Julie could see customers coming and going. As a way to draw people into the store, the Flagg Gallery also carried a line of art supplies and stationery. Vanessa generally thought the small sales were a nuisance, but she greeted these customers as enthusiastically as her major business clients. Julie smiled as she looked on. If she only had half of Vanessa's poise and confidence, she would be ecstatic.

She stared at the piece of paper in front of her and tried to concentrate on titles.

four

Julie looked at the image in the mirror and saw a stranger. Could that face really be hers?

Wisps of blond hair curled softly forward and highlighted her cheekbones and blue eyes. The back was cut in a chic streak at her shoulder, the split ends obliterated. Not a hair was out of place. Julie was afraid to move.

"Don't you like it?" the nervous hairdresser asked.

"It's great!" Julie assured her. "It's so. . .sophisticated."

"You said you wanted something special."

"I know. . .but the show is two days away. It'll never look this good when I fix it myself."

"Come back in that afternoon for a styling." The hairdresser unfastened the oversized bib around Julie's shoulders and shook the loose hair to the floor.

"Maybe I will." Julie stood up tentatively, still afraid to disturb her hair. She walked stiffly toward the cash register.

She paid for her haircut and moved cautiously down the street to her car. She could not suppress the impulse to touch her hair lightly and protectively. Hanging from the hook in the back seat was her new black gown, now a perfect fit on her tallish, slender frame. The shoes were in a box on the floor. Everything seemed to be coming together well.

Julie glanced at her watch. She barely had time to dash back to Leed House for some fresh clothes before meeting Larry for dinner. She unlocked the driver's door and lowered herself gingerly into the seat.

Winding her way on the streets of Seabridge, Julie marveled at how fond she had become of this town. It was not just her grandmother's town any longer. It had become her own. After a year and a half, she was still considered an outsider by the oldtimers, and she probably always would be. Della and Larry faced the same stigma. But having come from a Seabridge family gave Julie a bit of credibility.

There were two elderly women in the little community church who claimed to remember her grandmother. One, whom everyone called Aunt Joanna, said she had been Julienne Leed's best friend when they were girls. Julie was not sure what to make of that claim. Aunt Joanna was ninety-six years old and fragile; her mind seemed clear but her speech was garbled and thick. But Julie knew from reading her grandmother's diary that she had indeed had a friend named Joanna. Aunt Joanna did not get out to church much, so Julie hardly ever saw her. A couple of times the old woman had looked at her and studied her face intently, as if she were witnessing the impossible. At those moments, Julie knew that her resemblance to her grandmother went beyond their names. This gave her an eerie sense of the past, even more than living in her grandmother's old room or sitting in the old family pew.

Julie pulled into the freshly paved parking lot behind Leed House. The small lot was a modern concession to the business of running an inn. Larry and Della had accepted its necessity for the convenience of guests, but they had located it in the back of the house rather than disturbing the view of the front of the house. This meant that guests frequently came and went through a side door.

Della, seated comfortably in the gazebo out back with a book, waved. Julie grinned as she returned the gesture. She was glad to see that Della had taken advantage of a free evening and was doing something she enjoyed immensely.

Not wanting to disturb Della, Julie let herself in the back door, carefully cradling her new dress. As usual, the kitchen was spotless, so it was not difficult to see the note on the center of the round oak table. Carefully, she slung her dress over one shoulder and picked up the note.

> *Julie,*
>   *Had to run into town for some last-minute*
> *errands. Can you meet me at Victor's at 6:15?*
> *Looking forward to hearing about your day.*
>   *Larry*

Victor's was an expensive restaurant prominently located on the town square. It catered to tourists in the mood to splurge, boasting fresh seafood and an extravagant salad bar. As far as Julie knew, Larry had never been there before. She had certainly not expected to dine in such elegance tonight. This required more than a quick freshening up. She checked her watch again and wondered what in the world she should wear to a place like Victor's.

                           ஊ

She pulled into the lot promptly at six-fifteen and scanned the area looking for Larry's familiar pickup truck. She spotted it parked in a far corner, away from other vehicles, as was Larry's habit. She eased her used station wagon in next to his truck and got out. As she walked toward the front door of the restaurant, she saw him: tall, dark, bearded, and dressed in a dark suit. She glanced down at her own clothing selection, a pale pink chiffon dress that she had owned for many years but worn only a few times. She was fairly sure Larry had never see it before.

"You look fantastic," he said as she drew closer to him.

"Thanks. You look pretty sharp yourself."

"I didn't know you were going to get a new haircut."

Julie smiled self-consciously and touched her hair gingerly. "It was your mother's idea. She saw it in a magazine and thought it was perfect for my face."

"She was right." Larry extended his hand and took hers. "Are you hungry?"

"Well, yes, but Larry, this place will cost a fortune. Are you sure you want to stay here? I don't mind if—"

"Yes, I'm sure. I'm in the mood for crab salad and fresh clams." He squeezed her hand. "Just relax."

"I'll try."

They entered the lobby. The maitre d' was ready for them immediately. "Your table is ready, Mr. Paxton."

Julie looked at Larry, impressed but amused. "I thought you had given up the sophisticated New York life."

"Not completely." At the cozy window table, he pulled out her chair and she sat down.

In the center of the small round table was an arrangement of fresh flowers, with a lone slender burgundy candle rising from the mound of pink petals. Their places were set with exquisite, blue-bordered china and delicately patterned crystal. The cloth napkins were folded so intricately that Julie was hesitant to undo the artwork. Across the room a string quartet played Mozart.

"Larry?" She leaned forward and whispered across the table.

"Yes?"

"Why are we here?"

"For dinner, of course."

"You know what I mean. Why such extravagance?"

"I didn't want to take the chance of waiting until tomorrow. You might get tied up with last-minute details for the show, and I wanted to be sure you had a chance to relax and celebrate the occasion."

"I don't know what to say. You've gone to so much trouble."

"Not really. I just made a phone call to reserve a table."

"Come on, Larry. You put on a suit! You never do that."

"I seldom have a reason to." He reached across the table for her hand. "Just relax, Julie. I want you to enjoy the evening. Just think of it as a minivacation."

"I'll try."

The waiter came and they ordered generous portions of food from appetizers to dessert. Larry was completely unconcerned about cost.

"We'll be eating for hours," Julie said when the waiter was gone.

"We've got time," Larry responded, unruffled. "Tell me about your day."

Julie smiled. Larry knew her well enough to know that she would want to babble on about every detail of the day, analyzing aloud as she went along. The fact that he would invite the process never ceased to astound her. Tonight, especially, she appreciated his calming, indulging presence.

"David found a frame for the *Triumph* painting," she began. "It's a solid oak frame that is at least a hundred years old."

"Then it should fit well with the subject of the painting."

"It does! He had it restored and refinished, and it's a beautiful combination. I'll have to pay him for it, though, if I want to keep it."

"You're still planning to keep that painting?"

"Absolutely."

He nodded with satisfaction. "I don't think you could live with yourself if you let that one go."

"You're right about that."

"But it's too beautiful not to be displayed somewhere. Have

you thought about that question?"

"No, not really. I guess—"

"How about hanging it at Leed House?"

"But you already have two of my paintings."

"It's a big house. I can't think of a more fitting subject to hang in the house. . .unless you're planning a portrait of the original Captain Leed himself."

Julie laughed. "That would be strictly out of my imagination, but maybe I'll consider it."

"I know Mom would love to have *Triumph* hanging in the house. It would just be a loan. If you ever changed your mind or left Leed House. . ."

He left his sentence unfinished, awkwardly. Julie looked down at the napkin in her lap.

Their relationship was sincere and affectionate. She cared deeply for Larry and knew that he reciprocated her feelings. Yet they had never discussed life outside of Leed House, or the possibility that one or both of them might go on to something else. It was easy to live the status quo, one day at a time, and not think about the fact that they had not bound themselves to each other in any formal way, or even an informal one.

Julie shrugged off the moment before it became too intense. "I would love to hang *Triumph* in Leed House. Right after the show."

"Great." He sounded satisfied. Was it just because of the painting, or was it because *Triumph* would keep Julie at Leed House? She was not quite sure.

They lingered in the restaurant for nearly three hours. Satiated with rich food and conversation, they finally rose from their chairs to leave.

Julie put her hand on her stomach and groaned slightly.

"Are you all right?"

"Stuffed. I should have stopped two hours ago."

Larry nodded. "Me too. How about a walk around the town square?"

"Sure, but there won't be much happening at this hour of the evening in the middle of October."

"Doesn't matter." He looked at her thin dress and bare arms. "But it will be cold."

"I have a sweater in the car. It doesn't exactly go with my outfit, but it's warm."

They retrieved the sweater and started their route along the old bricked roads where vehicles were not allowed. Holding hands, they walked in silence for a few minutes. Julie grew wistful, remembering scenes from her grandmother's diary.

"My grandmother used to walk here with your grandfather, you know," she said.

"I remember. From the diary. They would meet here in the middle of the night sometimes."

"That's right."

"I can't imagine that her parents would have approved."

Julie shook her head. "I'm sure they never knew."

"It is strange to be here, in a funny way. As if life has come full circle. I never even knew my grandfather had been in Seabridge until I read the diary, and now here I am."

"He wasn't here long. . .just long enough for my great-grandparents to chase him away."

"I'm sure he was trying to do the right thing when he left. After all, if he hadn't left, you and I wouldn't be here now, would we?"

"I suppose not. We wouldn't be at all. We'd be other people, or something."

They continued in silence. Larry's words echoed in Julie's mind. *As if life has come full circle.* She looked at Larry's profile in the moonlight and wondered what it had been like for her grandmother to meet Lorenzo Scorzo here all those years ago, a teenager defying her parents for the man she loved. Who would have imagined that the grandchildren of the separated pair would now be following the same path, holding hands and walking in the moonlight?

I do care for Larry, Julie told herself silently. *Maybe I even love him. But would I still feel this way if he were not the grandson of Lorenzo Scorzo? Would I still care for him if life were not coming full circle by the crossing of our lives?* Julie had asked herself this question before. It remained unanswered.

Larry squeezed her hand, and she returned the gesture. They stood where the old stone fountain was.

"Somebody should get this going again," Julie said. "It adds such character to the town square. It's a shame it doesn't run regularly."

"Time changes things, even in Seabridge," Larry replied. He tilted his head back and pondered the black sky. "Look at the stars," he said.

"At least those don't change," Julie said. She tightened her grip on Larry's hand for balance as she, too, looked upward. Even sharing the night sky with a bright moon, the stars were spectacular.

"Have you ever painted the night sky?" Larry asked.

"No. I've thought about it, but I don't quite have a handle on it. It's too awesome to comprehend," Julie answered.

"But you do such beautiful things with light. The light of the stars is a perfect subject for you."

For the second time in one day, she was reminded of her own fascination with light. She painted light because it felt natural. Was there a deeper reason? And what did it have to do with faith?

He nudged her to stand in front of him and he put his hands

on her shoulders and his face next to hers and looked over her left shoulder.

She was grateful to be able to lean against him more securely. The impenetrable night sky always made her dizzy.

He kissed her cheek. "Are you warm enough?" He massaged her shoulders slightly.

"Ummm." She turned her face toward his. "Thanks for tonight, Larry. You were right. I needed a break before the next few days."

"It was my pleasure." He kissed her lips now, and she turned to face him fully and return his affection.

five

"How long have you been sitting out here?" Della's voice broke Julie's transfixed stare.

Slowly Julie turned her head and saw Della stepping into the gazebo. The morning sun silhouetted Della with a gray-ish, blurred outline.

"That depends," Julie said. "What time is it now?"

"It's almost seven o'clock."

"Then I've been out here about an hour."

Della dropped down on the wooden bench next to where Julie was huddled with an afghan around her shoulders and a sketch pad in her lap.

"It was still dark an hour ago."

"But I knew the sun would be up soon and I wanted to catch the light."

Della looked over Julie's shoulder at the drawing. Julie had been working on the intricate latticework and the playfully boxing shadows of the surrounding trees.

"That's an ambitious drawing for so early in the day."

Julie continued gently shading one corner of the page. "I just felt like doing it."

"I would think you would have every inch of this gazebo memorized," Della said. "Why haven't you ever painted it?"

"I've wanted to. I have two dozen sketches of it, at least."

"What's holding you back?"

"I want to capture the leisure era of lawn parties and tree climbing and fancy dresses. . .the way things were when my great-grandfather built this gazebo."

"Kids still climb trees," Della observed, "and wear fancy clothes."

"I know. But people hardly speak to their neighbors anymore, much less give lawn parties and let a bunch of people trample their grass."

"Things are different now," Della conceded. She turned and looked at Julie. "Why did you come out here so early?"

Julie shrugged. "Couldn't sleep."

"Too excited?"

"Nervous would be a better description."

"Well, I can certainly understand that. After all, this show is a major event in your life. It could be a real breakthrough in your career. Who knows who will come? David placed notices in the New York magazines, didn't he? I'm sure he must have. In fact, I'm sure I saw a photocopied notice on the counter at the gallery. He's so efficient; he would never overlook something like that. Isn't it wonderful that he has taken you under his wing?"

As Della rattled on, Julie tried to keep up, suddenly put at ease by this familiar kind of interaction with a friend who liked to talk too much. Most of what Della had to say was true, but when she got excited, she spoke almost faster than she could think.

"David has everything under control," Julie interjected. Over the last two years, Julie had learned that politely waiting for an opportunity could be futile. It was better just to jump right in. But Della did not hear her this time. Another paragraph spewed out.

"Meeting David has been wonderful for you, hasn't it? He's so respected all over New England. He works with only the best quality of artists, you know. That should tell you something right there, that he would even want to represent your work. So for him to arrange a show for you, well, it's absolutely spectacular. I just know it's going to be wonderful."

"I hope so."

"I'm talking too much again, aren't I?" Della swallowed hard and pressed her lips together. "You've got to speak up. Don't let me dominate the conversation like that."

Julie laughed. "It's all right. I'm not sure I can even carry on a coherent conversation today anyway."

"You really are nervous. Everything is going to be fine, Julie. You'll sell lots of paintings and get great reviews and people will be knocking down your door trying to commission portraits."

Julie laughed again. "That's certainly a nice dream. Then I can open my own studio, invest my incredible earnings, live off the interest, and paint for the rest of my life like an eccentric hermit."

"Of course you can."

"Or, I could end up on the street corner, begging people to buy my sketches so I have enough money to get home to Illinois and move back in with my parents."

"Don't be ridiculous," Della chastised. "That's not going to happen. You won't have to go home a failure. You can just live in the tower room for the rest of your life and no one will ever know."

Julie looked at Della sideways. "Now that's a pretty picture. Painter held prisoner."

Della patted Julie's knee. "Stop thinking such morbid thoughts. But stay out here as long as you want to. Finish your drawing."

"It's time to get breakfast started, isn't it?"

"I can handle it. I insist that you stay out here and relax. Finish your drawing. Come to breakfast when you hear the bell."

"Nonsense. I'll come in and help."

Della stood up. "I forbid it. You need to keep your mind focused on your art while you get ready for the show. You shouldn't spend the day doing ordinary housework."

Julie knew she was outranked so she recanted. "Okay, but as soon as the show is over, things go back to normal."

"We'll just see." Della turned and started walking away before Julie could argue further.

Julie picked up her sketch pad again and examined her work. It was acceptable, but not noteworthy. In her mind she experimented with improvements. She had done better sketches of the gazebo many times. Still, perhaps there would be something from it that she could incorporate into a whimsical garden painting someday. She would not throw it away.

Julie rarely threw away any of her sketches. She firmly believed there was something to be learned even from a poor effort. Though she would never let anyone else see them, she kept the mediocre drawings and half-done canvases in a secure but secret place. They pressed her on to do better the next time. Some of her best paintings had come out of the determination not to be discouraged by a failed effort. She jokingly referred to this menagerie of art as "The Worst of J. L. Covington." She refused to show them to anyone, not even Larry, who was her strongest supporter.

Gradually, Julie became conscious of an oncoming car engine. The sound seemed odd so early in the morning. Shivering in the morning chill, she gathered the afghan around her shoulders more tightly and turned her head toward the sound. A small foreign sports car pulled into the small parking lot at the back of the house. Julie had a clear view, and nothing could have surprised her more.

Vanessa Parker turned off the engine of her car and sat still. Julie waited for Vanni to open the door and get out; then she could greet her and find out what had brought her to Leed

House so early in the morning. In fact, what had brought her to Leed House at all? As far as Julie could remember, Vanni had been to the house only once before, for a surprise birthday party that Della had thrown for Julie. Although Julie had been to Vanessa's apartment often, Vanni always acted like it was out of her way to come by Leed House, and she seldom did. It had become a joke between them: How long could Vanessa avoid visiting where Julie lived? How many excuses could she come up with. Vanessa was very creative at dodging invitations. So why was she here now?

Julie was more than curious. Vanni still had made no effort to get out of the car. She simply sat behind the steering wheel, as if she were waiting for something. Julie could not imagine what would make Vanessa do what she was doing. Julie considered approaching her friend, but something told her to sit still for a few more minutes. On the bench, hidden by the lattice of the gazebo, she was out of sight of anyone in the parking lot.

The side door of Leed House opened, and Dayton Edwards emerged. He walked directly to Vanessa's car, placed his palms on the side panel, and leaned down toward the driver. The window opened about three inches. Vanessa and Dayton were talking; Julie could see that much. But she could hear nothing. They were talking quietly and she was too far away. Curious beyond measure, she moved silently to a spot where she could get a clearer view.

Julie did not know that Dayton and Vanni even knew each other. Dayton had been in town less than a week; for part of that time, Vanni had been on one of her sales trips, and Julie had not seen Dayton anywhere near the gallery. How could the two of them have met? Yet clearly they knew each other, and the meeting had been prearranged.

Dayton seemed his usual casual self, with relaxed posture

and comfortable clothing. He leaned on the car as if it were his own and smiled pleasantly at the occupant. But Vanessa was nervous about something. From her new position Julie could now see Vanni's face. She was not returning Dayton's smiles; the stony composure of her face never flinched. The window was open only as far as required for the conversation, no farther. Whatever the reason for this encounter, Vanessa was not enjoying it. Once again Julie stifled an impulse to make her presence known, if for nothing else than to come to the rescue of her friend.

But did Vanessa need rescuing? Julie could not be sure. As sociable as Vanni was, she could have had a hundred reasons for talking to Dayton Edwards. If that were the case, though, she should be smiling. Vanessa always smiled. It was part of the way she won people over so quickly. From Julie's perspective, Vanessa Parker did not look very interested in winning over Dayton Edwards.

Just then Dayton slapped the top of the car emphatically. Julie jumped involuntarily as he turned and went back into the house. Julie flew into action. She had sat still long enough, she decided. She would talk to Vanessa. Quickly Julie slipped through the archway of the gazebo so that she was in plain view. She waved her arm broadly to catch Vanessa's attention and hurried toward the parking lot.

This time Vanessa rolled the window all the way down.

"Good morning, Julie! How is the artist of the day?" Her voice bore no trace of the strain Julie had seen in her face only a moment ago.

"I'm okay," Julie answered cautiously. "What brings you to Leed House?" Perhaps Vanessa would tell her what was going on.

"I wanted to check up on you, of course."

"Oh?"

"Sure. David and I worked late last night. He's worried about you. He's afraid he has put you under too much stress."

"I'm a little nervous, but I'm fine."

"That's what I told him. But just to put his mind at ease, I promised him I would check on you first thing in the morning. So I thought I might as well just stop by on my way into the gallery, even though coming here is against personal policy." She flashed a smile at Julie.

"It's not really on your way," Julie countered, undistracted. "You live on the other side of town."

"But at least now I don't have to make a separate trip."

Julie nodded, though she was not convinced.

"So are you really all right?" Vanessa pressed on. "David wants to be sure you're in top form tomorrow night."

"I'll be fine. I just want to get opening night over with."

"That's always the worst part."

"Would you like some breakfast?" Perhaps if she could keep Vanessa at Leed House, Julie could get some real information from her.

Vanessa shook her head. Her dark waves rippled through the air. "I have a million things to do. Gotta go."

"You can tell David that I'll come by the showroom later this morning."

"I think he wants you to relax."

"Everybody wants me to relax!" Julie exclaimed, agitated. "But I need to stay busy. So I'll come and see what needs to be done."

"That's fair enough. You are the featured artist, after all." Vanessa raised her hand to the ignition. "Now that I know you're okay, I'd better get going myself. For the record, technically I didn't actually come inside Leed House."

Julie could not help smiling this time.

"See you later," Vanessa said, putting her car in gear.

"Goodbye." Julie stepped back as Vanessa backed up and pulled out of the lot. She could not be sure Vanessa was lying to her. Perhaps she had told David she would check on Julie. Why would Vanessa lie to her? Julie genuinely believed her friendship with Vanni was honest and mutual. The idea that Vanni was intentionally deceiving her was horrifying. Desperately, Julie wanted to believe Vanessa was simply checking up on her. But it seemed a very thin story, and it did not explain the encounter with Dayton Edwards.

The breakfast bell rang just then. Julie shuffled toward the house, her brow furrowed in mystery. When Julie reached the dining room, she saw that Della had set a place for her at the guest table.

"Here she is now," Larry said cheerfully.

All the guests were seated already and turned their heads. She felt foolish entering the room dressed in baggy sweats with an afghan over her shoulder. Self-consciously she tried to slick back a stray hair and swiftly discarded the afghan into an empty corner chair.

"Good morning, everyone." She tried to sound calm and cheerful and fought the impulse to bolt from the room.

"Julie, I'm so excited about seeing your paintings tonight." Mary Ellen Ventura was beginning another day with her usual gushing enthusiasm.

"I hope you'll enjoy them," Julie said meekly as she picked up her fork.

Lisa Butler spoke up. "I've seen the flyers up in all the store windows. We were planning to head back to the boat today and pull out of port, but I've convinced Theo we should see the show first."

"I'm flattered that you would change your plans for me. I hope you're not inconvenienced."

"It's just a new level of shopping for her," Theo Butler said lightheartedly as he heaped scrambled eggs on his plate. "Have you painted anything that would hang nicely while being tossed on the waves?"

Dayton Edwards reached for a warm roll and the butter. "I've been talking to people around town who have seen your work and they say it's wonderful."

"Thank you." *To whom had he spoken?* Julie wondered. *Was there a link between her paintings and Dayton's conversation with Vanessa?*

"How about you, Mr. Lamp?" Dayton said. "Are you staying for the show?"

"My business will conclude late today," Mr. Lamp said stiffly. "I'm afraid I won't be able to see the show, Miss Covington, but may I extend my congratulations to you?"

"Thank you."

"Perhaps another time."

"Of course," Julie said politely.

"I'm about to wrap things up, too," Dayton said, "but I don't have to rush off. I'm glad to have an excuse to stay another day or two in this charming old house."

From there the breakfast conversation turned to historical tidbits about the house and the Leed family. Larry fielded most of the questions, while Julie ate silently. She watched Dayton Edwards steadily. He looked just as he did every morning, eating voraciously and teasing the breakfast conversation into comaraderie.

Julie would not be satisfied until she had some answers to her questions. She determined to talk to Vanessa directly later in the day.

six

"No, not there! Lower. The bottoms of the frames must be aligned perfectly." David Flagg barked orders at two young men in coveralls and left no room for discussion of his point. His sleeves were rolled up and his hands planted authoritatively on his hips.

"Take it down and hang it again," David insisted. "A half-inch error will destroy the effect of the entire display."

Julie stood in the doorway of the showroom that adjoined the shop, watching David at work. He was a perfectionist. If he could not do a job right, he did not do it at all. Perhaps this was why the Flagg Gallery had built up such a reputation throughout New England as an excellent showcase of art. Julie appreciated his perfectionism; she could see from across the room that he was right. The alignment was off on one wall, and it distracted her eye from the paintings themselves. The young men removed the offending frame and measured again.

David was at last satisfied with the way the painting was hung and turned around looking for his clipboard and checklist. A small table in the middle of the room served as his command post. He finally noticed Julie leaning against the wall.

"Hello, Julie. Do you need something?" He was his usual businesslike self.

"No, not really," she answered. "I just wanted to see how things were shaping up. It looks nice." She walked toward the center of the room where he stood.

"As you can see, about half of the paintings are hung. If these guys would be just a little more precise in their measuring, we wouldn't have to do everything twice. Things would go a lot faster."

"Still, it's coming along."

"Yes, I suppose it is. We should finish hanging everything today."

"When do the caterers come?"

David glanced at his watch. "Right after lunch, in about an hour. I hope we can keep out of their way."

"Maybe they could come tomorrow morning, just to set up tables and chairs, then come back later with the food."

"I suggested that. Mrs. Thurston insisted they had to do the tables today." His attention shifted again to a young man wandering idly with a painting. "No, over there, on the far wall," he called out to the worker. With his clipboard tucked under one arm, he left Julie. "Haven't you looked at the plans? The paintings are all clearly labeled. Which one do you have there?" David's voice trailed away as he moved to the far end of the room.

Julie stood in awe of the room. She had been to dozens of art showings and this one was comparatively small. Yet it was impressive. David had offered her a show more than a year ago. Then he had proceeded to push her to produce as much as she could in preparation for the show. In the end, though, there were some paintings she refused to exhibit. . . some older ones that were too amateurish, some recent ones that were done in too much of a hurry. While she appreciated what David was trying to do for her, she resented working against a deadline. Vanessa always reminded her that she had agreed to the deadline a long time ago. Still, Julie was not used to outside pressure. At one point she had expected David to pull out of the show completely because she did not have enough work to exhibit. But he hadn't done that. He had insisted that even a small show would be worth the effort.

On the other hand, Julie was surprised at how much there was to display. She had not kept track numerically of how many paintings David was planning to use. He had made some attractive groupings. The effect was a nice collection, showing several different styles with which she had been experimenting. Generally, there were seasonally distinct landscapes, a few recent attempts at seascapes, and a series of portraits, both people she knew and strangers whose faces had come to her imagination. She glanced around the room looking at the track lighting. David obviously knew what he was doing. Every painting received just the right amount of light from just the right distance. The caterers would provide a tasty array of hors d'oeuvres selected from a sophisticated menu, and Vanessa had selected a stack of compact discs of classical music to set the atmosphere.

It would be a good show. Even if she did not sell a single painting, the experience was one Julie would never forget.

The double entry doors crashed open and a graying, middle-aged woman with a severe expression entered the room, followed by two more young men carrying an eight-foot-long table.

"Mr. Flagg," she called out curtly.

At the other end of the room, David wheeled around.

"Mrs. Thurston. You're early."

"Yes, we have quite an agenda today. We will leave the tables for you now, but I'm afraid we haven't time to set them up." The two young men propped the table up against a wall next to the door.

"Tomorrow perhaps?"

"It would be so helpful if you could have your young men place them appropriately."

"Mrs. Thurston, we agreed—"

She cut him off. "I have no time for this discussion, Mr. Flagg. I have to get these tables out of my truck today. I shall be back tomorrow night one hour before the show begins. I will leave the tablecloths, also. If you would please see that the tables are set up." She turned and walked away curtly, through the doorway.

The men were back with another table, which they stacked against the first one. They made six more trips, leaving a total of four tables, thirty-six chairs, and a rack of freshly pressed table linens.

When they were gone for good, David slammed his clipboard against the edge of a display board. "I can't believe she did that. We have a clear contract for services."

Julie was speechless. "Well. . .we'll just have to. . .I can stay and help with things."

"That's not the point. This is her responsibility. It's not my fault that she overbooked herself. That's the last time I use Thurston's to cater anything."

The door opened again and Vanessa Parker entered. "What happened in here, David? I just saw Mrs. Thurston looking like she'd had her face pickled."

"She has reneged on our agreement, that's what happened. She wants us to do the tables ourselves. Don't ever book her again."

"I'll take care of the tables, David," Vanessa said calmly. She handed him a paper. "Here. This fax just came for you."

David grabbed the paper and scanned it. His face paled as he read it more carefully the second time.

"What is it, David?" Julie asked anxiously. She had never seen such an expression on his face.

"It's my mother," he said quietly. "A stroke."

Vanessa gasped. "Is she. . . ?"

"She's alive, but in critical condition. My sister thinks I should come right away."

"Then you must go," Vanessa said.

David looked around the room and sighed. "But what about all this? The show opens tomorrow night."

Vanessa pried the clipboard out of his hands and riffled through the pages it held. "You have everything already planned. I'll just follow your instructions and everything will get done."

"And I can help," Julie interjected. "For once your habit of writing everything down will have some usefulness."

"I can be back for tomorrow night."

"Don't think about that right now," Julie said. "Go see your mother and we'll just take it one step at a time."

"I only have to go to Vermont. I will be back tomorrow night." He pulled a pen out of his pocket and snatched the clipboard back from Vanessa. "The top sheets are the drawings for how the paintings should be hung. I want you to check on the food this afternoon. I don't care how busy Mrs. Thurston is, I want to know that exactly what we ordered will be delivered on time. Betty is running the shop today and she has arranged people to act as hostesses, but you'll have to check with her about that. The price list is in my left desk drawer, just in case I don't make it back. Don't let anyone bargain you down. I want you to call—"

"David," Vanessa said quietly as she put her hand on his arm. "It's all here. I'll look after the details."

"You've never run a show by yourself before."

"But I've watched you put one together half a dozen times. Don't worry. Go see your mother."

David sighed heavily and turned to Julie. "Sorry, Julie. I have no choice."

She shook her head. "I wouldn't want you here under these

circumstances."

"I will see you tomorrow night." With that, David turned and crossed the room and left.

Julie turned to face Vanessa. "You're in charge, but I want to help," she said.

"This isn't what you were supposed to be doing today, but I suppose I could use an extra pair of hands." She handed the clipboard to Julie. "Here, take this. Keep an eye on those guys down there and make sure they're getting the paintings up right. I need to go talk to Betty in the shop. I won't be long."

Left standing alone in the middle of the room, Julie suddenly felt anxious. What if David did not make it back? Until he had left, she had not realized how much she depended on him for a successful show. Would Vanessa know what she was doing when the show opened? *Of course she will,* Julie told herself. *Vanni is a professional.*

Julie forced herself to focus on the drawings in her hand and to match them with what was up on the walls. So far everything matched the plan. The workmen were working steadily, measuring more carefully now after David's lecture. When Vanessa returned, she was not alone.

"Dayton!" Julie said. "What are you doing here?"

He grinned at her. "I stopped in the shop to see if I could catch a preview of the show and I overheard your friend here saying that Mr. Flagg had a family emergency and had to leave. She sounded like she could use some help, so of course I volunteered."

"Well, thank you." Julie looked at Vanessa, who said nothing. She appeared much less enthusiastic about Dayton's offer to help than he did. Vanni would not meet her glance. Julie's anxiety returned. What was really going on here?

Standing up straight with his chin in the air, Dayton

inspected the room. "Great lighting," he said. "And nice wide aisles so you can stand back and look at a painting properly." He started pacing around slowly, looking at paintings, his hands locked together behind his back.

Julie did not know what to say. She had found Dayton Edwards a pleasant enough guest at Leed House and had enjoyed a few humorous banterings. He had the sort of personality that was difficult to resist, not unlike Vanessa. But why was he really in Seabridge? Why did he have so much time on his hands? She supposed she should be grateful Dayton was available. They did need help.

"Are you sure he has time to help?" she whispered to Vanessa. "Doesn't he have any business meetings, or something?"

Vanni shrugged. "He says he's free all day. I tried to turn him down, but he wouldn't take no for an answer. Claims he's already an ardent fan of your work because of what he has seen at Leed House."

"There were two paintings at Leed House," Julie said, mystified. "But I brought those over here the first day Dayton was in town. He hardly had a chance to see them."

"Then they must have made quite an impression."

Her curiosity rising, Julie wanted to ask Vanessa about that morning's encounter with Dayton in the driveway. "Vanni," she started. "This morning, when you came to Leed House. . . Why were you really there?"

"I told you," Vanessa responded, flipping the pages on the clipboard. "To check on you."

"But—"

"We'd all better get to work." Vanessa cut Julie off, as if she knew what was coming. Her voice sounded unusually flat and unnecessarily loud. "Are you ready, Mr. Edwards? There will be plenty of time to look later."

"Right," Dayton responded and started back toward Julie and Vanessa. "What's first?"

"Julie, you keep on top of the hangings." Vanessa started toward the caterer's tables. "Mr. Edwards, if you would help me with these tables."

"Certainly." Dayton's voice was unnecessarily cheerful. Julie did not like the feeling in her stomach.

seven

I think you should get out of here," Vanessa's voice was authoritative and Julie took her seriously. She looked at her watch.

"Well, I did have a couple of things I was going to do," conceded Julie.

"I should never have let you stay this late in the day. You'll get bags under your eyes. If you're not looking fabulous tomorrow night, it will be all my fault for working you so hard today. I would never forgive myself."

Although Vanessa's words were typical for her personality, the shine was missing from her voice. All day long, Julie had been looking for another opportunity to discuss Dayton Edwards, but none had arisen. Now Julie was getting distracted and had convinced herself it was not important to pursue the question right now.

"If I don't look fabulous," she said, "it will be because I look like myself." Self-consciously, Julie twirled a strand of hair.

"Cut that out," Vanni said sternly. "The haircut looks great, the dress is beautiful. You'll be a smashing success."

"I hope so. And I hope David makes some money off of all this. He's put so much work into it. Both of you have."

"Don't let David intimidate you. This is your show. Remember that."

"I'll try."

"Now get out of here."

"Are you sure everything is taken care of?"

"Dayton has done a great job with the heavy work. And I can handle the thinking. Go on. Go pamper yourself. Take a long soak in the tub or something."

"Mmm. That would be wonderful."

"I don't want to see your face around here again until tomorrow night."

Julie laughed. "Okay. I'll do my best to stay away."

She gathered her things together and turned to go. Vanessa had already started on the next job on her list. Julie quietly slipped out of the building.

Out on the street, she squinted in the autumn sunlight. In the middle of the afternoon, the day had not yet begun to dim. A crispness in the air gave a hint of the season to come. Wind rushed through the trees, startling Julie and making her look up at the sound. A rash of leaves was shaken loose and fell to the sidewalk in front of her, splaying in a delicate formation. Mary Ellen Ventura was right; the colors were spectacular. Maybe next year she would do a series of paintings depicting the changing seasons, Julie decided. She would have to scout around for just the right location. Pondering this project, she wandered up the street toward where she had left her car parked.

With a gasp, she almost dropped the canvas bag slung over her shoulder. She stood in front of her car and let her mouth drop open. The front left corner was crumpled deeply inward and the headlight was smashed. The bumper was nearly sheared off; it hung precariously by one screw. In disbelief she stooped to look more closely. The picture only got worse. The fender was jammed into the tire and would have to be pried loose before the car could be driven.

Letting her shoulders sag, Julie slumped against the side of the car and tried to think of what to do. Her instinct was to run back to the showroom and tell Vanessa and use the phone there, but she stifled that impulse. Vanessa had her hands full right now. It would be better if she just found another phone and called the police.

She scanned the street looking for a pay phone, but saw none. Past all the small businesses, antique stores, and crafts shops of Seabridge, her eyes came to rest on the community church at the end of the block. If Charles Brooke were in, the church would be open. That would probably be the easiest thing to do, she decided. Reluctantly she admitted to herself that she did not want to deal with this particular crisis on her own. She shuffled up the street.

The side door of the church, the one outside the pastor's study, was unlocked. Tentatively, Julie pulled it open and poked her head inside.

"Hello? Pastor Brooke?"

"In here!"

She followed his voice and found him in the church's tiny library.

"Hi, Pastor Brooke."

"I've told you a hundred times to call me Charles."

"Sorry. Hi, Charles."

He put down the book he was reading. "What's the matter? You look distressed."

"I didn't think it showed."

"So something is wrong?"

"Nothing major. It's just my car."

"Broke down?"

"Smashed up."

"What?" She had his full attention now.

"I left it parked on the street, outside the showroom, a few hours ago. I just came out and saw that it had been hit. Can I use the phone?"

"Certainly."

Charles led the way to the church office. He dialed the police then handed Julie the phone. She gave the facts as accurately as she could, listened to instructions, then hung up.

"They're sending someone to look at it," she reported.

"Surely the other car must have been damaged, too. Perhaps they'll find the driver that way."

"I have to go wait. By the car, I mean."

"I'll go with you."

"I didn't mean to inconvenience you."

"No problem." He picked up his sport jacket from the back of a chair. "Let's go."

As she passed through the doorway, she felt the light touch of his hand on her back. Her breathing calmed, and she felt reassured.

They walked back to the car and Charles inspected the damage for himself. "Whoever hit you was driving a green car."

"Can you tell that?"

"Sure. See for yourself. Green paint all over your fender."

Julie looked and agreed with his conclusion. "So we're looking for a damaged green car. Not exactly a lot to go on."

"You'd be surprised." Charles glanced around. "Did you check with any of the storekeepers to see if they heard anything?"

"No, I just came straight to the church to use the phone."

"Just as well. The police can do that."

"Do you really think they'll find the other driver?"

He shrugged. "Maybe not. But they'll try. Have faith."

She blushed at his reference to her lack of faith and smiled awkwardly.

"Sorry," he said. "Sometimes those things just slip out of my mouth."

Julie shrugged. "Well, it would make a nice practical experiment in faith."

"Faith is never practical," Charles said, "For most people, it's the last recourse they try. But the notion of experimenting with faith is intriguing. In fact, I can just see it now: A painting by Julie Covington entitled, *Faith Experiment.*"

Julie laughed. "Is that a subtle way of asking me if I've made up my mind about the painting for the church?"

"Let's just call it a friendly reminder."

"I haven't had a lot of time to think about it since I ran into you yesterday."

Charles leaned casually against the passenger side of her car. "No, of course not. I didn't expect you to. Not till after the show."

Julie glanced into the back seat of the car. "Actually, my sketch pad is in the car. Maybe if I show you how weak the drawings are, you'll reconsider the commission."

"Nonsense. Bring on the sketches."

Julie opened the back door and retrieved her sketch book. They leaned against the side of the car, side by side, as they looked at her drawings. Their shoulders and heads nearly touched as they leaned in toward the sketch book.

"I was thinking of a picture from the life of Christ," Julie explained as she flipped quickly through several sketches. "Or maybe a crisis in the life of one of the disciples."

Charles examined the drawings again, this time more slowly. He did not speak. Julie could hear his slow, even breathing and waited for his opinion. Self-consciously, she realized their shoulders were rubbing now and stepped away.

"Those are nice and safe topics." he finally said..

She looked at him, puzzled.

Charles continued. "I don't mean to be irreverent, and a picture from the life of Christ would inspire many people."

"But it's not what you want?" Julie flipped the sketch book shut.

Charles shook his head. "More importantly, it's not what you want to paint. I don't want this painting to be something that belongs on a drugstore calendar. I want it to really be yours. Maybe *Faith Experiment* is not such a bad idea."

"That's not a very concrete image to work with."

"Faith is not concrete."

Julie twisted her lips to one side as she considered his statement. "Maybe I could do something with that theme. But it might be more abstract than the church people want."

"We'll cross that bridge when we come to it."

Another voice broke in on their conversation.

"Julie! Charles!" It was Larry, half a block away.

Julie scrambled to throw the sketch book back into the car. "Don't say anything," she whispered to Charles. "I don't want anyone to know about this idea."

"What are you two doing here, standing in the street?" Larry Paxton looked from Julie to Charles and back again, curious.

"Julie's car was hit," Charles explained honestly. "We're waiting for the police to come and make an accident report."

"Are you all right, Julie?" Larry asked anxiously, reaching out to her with affectionate concern.

"Perfectly fine. I wasn't in the car when it happened." She nodded toward the front of the car. "Front left."

Larry circled the car and looked at the damage. "Whoever hit this must have been going pretty fast. It's sure not just a fender bender. You can't even drive this home, Julie."

"I didn't think so."

"Look, I have to run up the street to the hardware store. I'll be right back. As soon as the police are done, we'll see about getting it towed and then I'll take you home."

"Thanks."

"Of all the times for something like this to happen. . .the day before your show."

"It does feel sort of unreal at the moment," Julie admitted.

Larry looked from Charles to Julie and back again. Julie took a step back, away from Charles.

"I'll be right back," Larry said, and then he headed up the block.

Charles and Julie hardly heard the engine of the police car as it pulled up behind them. Officer Dan Rakes emerged with a clipboard full of official forms and shuffled toward them.

"Good afternoon, Charles," Officer Rakes said.

"Good afternoon, Dan." Charles nodded his head toward the car. "Hit and run. Green car, going pretty fast, I'd say."

Dan chuckled. "Playing detective these days, Charles?"

"I'll match my deductive skills against yours anytime."

"You gotta quit reading those detective novels." He started sketching the location of the car and writing a description of the damage.

"Think you can find the other driver?" Charles probed.

Dan shrugged. "If it was someone local, we might. If it was a tourist, they'll be long gone by now."

"I was afraid of that," Julie moaned. Her head was starting to hurt. She put her hand up to her left temple.

"You all right?" Charles asked.

She nodded. "It's been a crazy day, that's all. First David has to leave because his mother is sick, and now this."

"David left?" Charles looked alarmed.

"His mother had a stroke. But Vanessa has everything under control."

Charles put his hand on her shoulder sympathetically. "Aw, Julie, what a rough day this has turned out to be."

She was comforted by his gesture, though her head continued to throb.

In another couple of minutes, Dan finished the paperwork. "Sign here," he said, thrusting the form at Julie. "I'll get my

Polaroid and take a few shots for evidence, then you can do what you like with the car."

When Dan was finished with the pictures and went away, Julie sighed deeply. "I don't know where to begin. Do you know a good body shop around here, Charles?"

"You don't have to decide right this minute. Why don't we go into the cafe across the street and get a cup of coffee?"

Julie was about to gratefully accept the invitation when she remembered Larry.

"But Larry will be looking for me," she said, glancing in the direction of the hardware store.

"Ah, yes." Charles looked mildly disappointed.

Julie was about to reconsider the offer; her head was pounding now.

"Oh no!" a voice boomed behind them. "What happened here?"

Julie whirled around to see Dayton Edwards staring at the front of her car.

"It's pretty obvious what happened," Charles said, extending his hand. "I don't believe we've met. I'm Charles Brooke."

Dayton shook his hand. "Dayton Edwards. I'm working temporarily at the gallery, helping to get Julie's show together." He turned back to the car.

"Wow, this is a mess, Julie."

She wished he would stop repeating the obvious; she did not respond to his statement.

"Well, Vanessa has me running an errand, so I shouldn't dawdle. Besides, it looks as if you are in good hands."

"Yes, I'll be fine. Thank you."

Dayton crossed the street just as Larry arrived back at the accident scene.

"Was that Dayton Edwards?" Larry asked.

"Yes. He's helping Vanessa out at the showroom."

"Doing what?" Larry was suspicious. His eyes followed Dayton's path down the block.

Julie shrugged. "Odds and ends. Whatever needs doing at this point."

"Why is he walking?"

"I suppose he doesn't have far to go."

"Where is his car?"

"How should I know?" Julie was getting irritable with the whole situation and just wanted to go somewhere and sit down.

Larry took his eyes off of Dayton and looked at Julie. "Doesn't Dayton drive a green car?" he asked.

eight

The green blob pulsed down the street absorbing trees, cars, bicycles, parking meters, even people into its slimy, jelly tentacles. Its distended belly wrenched from side to side. Surging unhindered through the historic town square, it was a powerful mass that no one dared challenge. Greasy residue defaced brick buildings two centuries old; windows smashed in the face of its erratic movements. At the beach, as it slithered toward the ocean, a lone young woman chased it and pounded against it, surprised to find it hard as wood. *Knock! Knock!*

She threw herself against it with all the force she could muster. *Knock! Knock!*

With a gasp, Julie woke from her dream. So far the night had not offered the soothing relaxation for which she had hoped.

Knock! Knock! She turned her head toward the door of her room. She had thought the dream was over.

"Julie! Wake up!" It was Della's urgent cry from the doorway.

Rubbing her eyes, Julie slung her feet over the side of the bed. It was too dark to be morning. What time was it? What was wrong?

"Julie!"

"I'm coming," she finally mumbled.

She pulled open the door to see Della standing in the hall looking more flustered than Julie had ever seen her.

"Julie, you have to get dressed. Right away." Della barged past Julie and scooped up a pair of jeans tossed over a chair.

Julie rubbed her eyes again. She could not concentrate on hearing and seeing at the same time. "Della, what's going on?"

"The police called."

"About my car? At this hour? What time is it?"

"Almost two-thirty. No, not the car. Something else. Quickly, get dressed."

A wave of panic rolled over Julie. "Della, what is it? Just say it."

Della took a deep breath. "There's been a break-in at the gallery."

Julie's mouth dropped open. "The shop or the showroom?" she asked weakly.

"The showroom."

Julie's eyes widened. "No!"

"Officer Rakes wants you down there to identify what's missing."

Julie thought she was going to be sick. She clenched her fists to keep from screaming. Someone had stolen some paintings. She ran one hand through her tousled hair and took the jeans from Della with the other. "I'll get dressed right away."

"Good. Larry will take you downtown."

Della turned and scurried back down the stairs. Julie scrambled into the jeans and a sweatshirt and followed.

ta

She held Larry's hand as they walked from his parked truck to the front door of the gallery in the middle of the night. The familiar signs and stores held no warmth tonight, no coastal town charm. As the knot in her throat grew, her grip on Larry's hand tightened. Bright lights shone from inside the gallery on an otherwise dim and quiet street. Dan Rakes and two other officers milled around the doorway.

"What's going on, Dan?" Larry asked.

"Sergeant Stubbs was on his routine check of the businesses on this block and he found the front door ajar."

"You mean it was open?" Julie asked incredulously.

"Unlocked and open."

"When did you discover this?" Larry asked.

"Just a few minutes ago. We called you right away."

"Did Stubbs see anything? Or anybody?"

"Nothing. As soon as the backup got here he turned on all the lights and had a good look around. I guarantee you there is nobody inside this building."

Larry squeezed Julie's hand and glanced at her. "It's okay," he said soothingly. "Let's just go in and have a look around ourselves."

"Miss Covington, are all the paintings displayed yours?"

"Yes, that's right."

"There are some paintings missing from their hooks. I need you to identify what they were."

Julie swallowed hard, barely able to believe this was happening. She nodded. "There's a list somewhere, too. Vanessa has it, I think. Or it might be in the office."

"Who is Vanessa?"

"Vanessa Parker. She works for the Flagg Gallery. David left her in charge yesterday."

"We tried to reach Mr. Flagg and there was no answer, either on the phone or in person."

"He had a family emergency. His mother. He had to go out of town."

"I see. So this Vanessa Parker was in charge?"

"Yes. David is going to try to get back for the show, but Vanessa was getting everything ready."

"She would have been responsible to lock up and so forth?"

"Yes, and I'm sure she did."

"Were you here when she left?"

"No, but she's fastidious about that kind of thing. She would never have left that up to anyone else."

"But you can't testify to that, can you? You didn't actually see her lock up."

"Well, no, but—"

"Do you know her address?"

Julie struggled to remember the street address, but the numbers would not form in her confused mind. "She lives in that apartment building at Simms and Randall. The old brick one. Top floor in the rear."

Rakes turned away. "Stubbs! Check out Vanessa Parker." He tore the sheet off his note pad and handed it to Stubbs.

"You can go on in." Rakes's voice was matter-of-fact.

Julie and Larry stepped inside the showroom and cautiously looked around it. The bright lights gave off a false warmth, a sense of security in which Julie would never again believe.

Everything was exactly as it should have been: paintings hung, caterer's tables in place, stereo system hooked up. The room was immaculate. But three hooks were starkly bare.

Julie gave a cry and put her fist to her mouth.

"What is it, Julie?" Larry said, following her line of sight with his eyes.

"*Triumph.* They took *Triumph*!"

"Are you sure?"

She pointed and nodded. "It should be right there!"

"Maybe it hasn't been hung yet."

"No, it was there. I saw it." She nearly flew across the room to stand before the empty hook.

"Please don't touch anything," boomed Dan Rakes's voice from the doorway. "Just look around and let me know what's missing."

Julie swallowed and breathed heavily, trying to keep from sobbing. She knew exactly what was gone. "Three paintings.

A large portrait of my grandmother and two summer land-scapes. They were part of a series. The rest are here."

"Anything else? Equipment? Papers?"

Julie looked around the room again. "No, they didn't touch the sound system—and that's worth a lot of money!" She turned to Larry and let him hold her against his chest. The tears came.

"It's not easy to hide a painting the size of *Triumph*," Larry said. "We'll find it, Julie, I promise."

She sniffled. "I don't understand. Why would anyone take my paintings? I'm not famous. They aren't really worth any-thing on the black market. It just doesn't make any sense."

She sniffled again and Larry handed her his handkerchief.

"No, it doesn't make sense," he agreed, stroking her head gently.

Officer Rakes approached them. "Miss Covington, do you have any reason to believe someone in particular is respon-sible for this?"

"What do you mean?" She stepped away from Larry and looked at Dan in disbelief.

"He wants to know if you have any enemies," Larry said bluntly.

"Enemies? Why would I have any enemies? As far as I know, I've never offended anyone in town. I have no idea who did this. . .or why!"

"No one has made any threats or strange comments?" Dan probed. "Perhaps something you didn't take seriously at the time?"

Julie shook her head emphatically. "I can't think of any-thing."

"Let's not forget about your car," Dan said.

"You think that was intentional?" Larry asked.

"I didn't this afternoon, but in light of this theft tonight, it could have been. It would be quite a coincidence for Miss Covington to be the target of two random crimes in one day, especially in this town."

Larry squeezed his grip around Julie's shoulders. "Do you think she is in any danger?"

"Physically? No, I doubt it."

Julie looked at Larry, unconvinced. "What if someone is out to hurt me?"

"I think someone does want to hurt you," Dan said, "but not physically. Somebody is harassing you for some reason. You're the only who can tell us why."

"But I don't know why!" she said vehemently.

"Take it easy," Rakes said.

Julie sighed and leaned back against Larry. The door opened and Stubbs came in.

"What did you find out?" Rakes barked.

"She lives there all right. But she wouldn't let me in. Kept the chain on the door."

"We'll get a warrant if we need one."

Julie was alarmed. "You don't seriously think Vanessa had anything to do with this, do you?"

"Can't rule anyone out at this point. She was the one responsible for security today. And it's clear that security was compromised." He turned back to Stubbs. "Why wouldn't she let you in?"

"Said she was very ill and it was impossible to come down here with me. I must say, she did look a little green in the face."

Julie's heart was beating faster now. This was not adding up. Vanessa had been fine earlier in the day. And even if she were sick, she would still come down to the showroom for an emergency like this one. Vanessa was fiercely loyal to the Flagg Gallery and never missed a day's work no matter how she felt. Julie kept silent.

Dan was talking again. "I want you to put a watch on Vanessa Parker. Make sure she doesn't leave that apartment. Then go back in the morning and ask how she's feeling."

"Right." Stubbs turned to go.

"According to our records this building has a security alarm system."

Julie nodded. "Yes. I don't really know how to use it, but I know where the panel is."

"Do you have any knowledge of a recent malfunction in the system?"

She shrugged. "That's not something David or Vanessa would need to tell me. But with the show I'm sure David would have wanted everything working perfectly."

"Well, either the system was not working, or this was an inside job."

"Inside job?"

"You know. Someone who works here pulled this stunt. Somebody who has frequent, easy access."

"But there's just David and Vanessa. And Betty Price. She helps out in the shop sometimes."

Rakes wrote down the name, Betty Price. He slapped his clipboard against his thigh and scanned the room. "My guess is that somebody knew exactly what they were doing. This was no ordinary break-in. They were after something quite specific." Turning back to Julie he asked, "Have you met any new people lately. . .said something to someone you don't know well. . .anything like that?"

Larry interjected, "She lives and works at a bed and breakfast inn. She meets new people every week."

"How well do you screen your guests?"

"What do you mean? If they can pay the charge, they stay in a room. We don't require security clearance."

"Anybody acting suspicious lately?"

Julie turned her palms up in frustration. "They're all strangers to me. How would I know if they are acting suspiciously?"

"Maybe they did something you did not expect. Lurking around. . .that sort of thing."

She thought of yesterday morning and Dayton Edwards's encounter with Vanessa.

"I saw one of the guests talking to Vanessa yesterday. I didn't realize they knew each other. Later she hired him to help with some of the heavy work around here."

Rakes was writing again. "What do you know about this guest?"

"Nothing, really. He's been at Leed House about four days."

"And he drives a green car," Larry added, "which I haven't seen around since the accident."

"Oh?" Rakes looked up. "We'll check into it. In fact, why don't you give me the names of everyone staying at the inn right now. Perhaps I'll drop in for breakfast."

"Is that necessary?" Larry asked. "It will alarm the guests. Not exactly good for business."

Rakes shrugged. "I have to talk to these people. You said yourself that you don't know much about them."

"Just don't make a public scene of it; that's all I'm asking."

Larry reluctantly began listing names and telling what he knew about each of the guests. As Julie listened to his descriptions, she realized how much they did *not* know about these people. They could have been in Seabridge for any reason at all. What were the Butlers really doing, going from town to town on their boat? Did they have a permanent address anywhere? And Mary Ellen was a bit strange most of the time, but was it just a ploy? Fenway Lamp had come and gone over the last few months but would not even say what kind of business he was in. And of course, there was Dayton Edwards, with his charming, winning smile. She really knew nothing about him, yet he seemed to have a keen interest in her.

"Well, we've taken prints from several places," Dan said when Larry finished the guest list. "We'll process those. I'm not hopeful anything will turn up. We do have the time frame narrowed down to between eleven o'clock at night to two o'clock in the morning."

"That's a pretty good stretch of time," Larry said.

Dan nodded. "It's the best we can do. You folks can go on home. Try to get some sleep. I'll see you in the morning."

nine

Julie and Larry did go home but they did not sleep. Della greeted them when they walked through the back door at four o'clock in the morning. As they sank into chairs around the antique table, she poured steaming mugs of coffee and set them before Julie and Larry. Julie gratefully gulped the coffee but was too distraught to talk coherently.

"*Triumph* is missing," Larry told his mother, and the three of them fell into a silent grief.

Gradually they began to converse. While Julie listened, Larry recounted for his mother everything that had transpired at the gallery.

"What about the show?" Della asked. "Is it in danger of being canceled?"

"I don't know," Julie answered. "I can't think straight about anything."

"I suppose it will be up to David," Larry speculated. "From a business perspective, he'll be affected, too. He may not want to proceed under these circumstances."

Julie sighed heavily. "Whatever he wants to do will be fine with me. I trust his judgment. I can't understand Vanessa, though. She was fine this afternoon. If she couldn't even come downtown for something like this, she must really be sick. If she's too sick to work the show. . . Well, I don't even want to think about that."

Della refilled their coffee cups. "How could anyone think you have any enemies?" she demanded. "Everybody who knows you thinks the world of you. They're proud to have you in Seabridge." Della clearly was agitated at the insinuation that Julie had offended anyone in the small town.

"Enemy is a strong word, Mom," Larry cautioned, although he had used it himself earlier. "We don't know for sure that there is anyone. But Dan Rakes was not ready to believe that the accident and the theft on the same day were coincidental."

They were thoroughly stumped.

At five-thirty Della stood up and stretched. "I'd better get started on breakfast, I guess. I don't feel much like catering to people right now, but I suppose I have to."

"I'll help," Julie said, rising to her feet.

Della considered this for a fraction of a second and then nodded silently. On this day she would not argue with Julie about anything. Together they made from scratch a batch of blueberry muffins and a large breakfast quiche. Julie mixed up a fresh pitcher of orange juice while Della set up the coffee urn.

"Julie, go on upstairs for a while," Della said at last, as she put the quiche in the oven.

"I won't be able to sleep."

"Just freshen up. I'll do the same. We can't greet our guests looking like this."

Julie nodded somberly and made her way up two flights of polished oak stairs to the tower room, her refuge. For the first time since she had moved into the room, she felt no comfort from its confines. After having the painting closest to her soul torn away from her, she would take nothing for granted.

Hoping to be revived physically at least, Julie opted for a long hot shower. When she emerged, she followed her morning habit and went to the window. Throwing open the shutters, she saw a brilliant morning. She was unprepared for the contrast with the dark sky she had come from a few hours ago. The day was clear and crisp, a perfect fall day.

It ought to be rainy and gray, she thought to herself. *How can the sun be shining on such a miserable day?*

She sank into the armchair near the window and stared out. Life in the neighborhood was undisturbed. The dogs yapped as usual, cars backed out of driveways as people left for work and school, another layer of leaves covered the ground. Everything appeared as it should be.

But everything was not as it should be. *Triumph* was gone. Apparently someone had a grudge against Julie. Although Larry was not ready to come to that conclusion, it was the only thing that made sense to Julie. It seemed an unsolvable mystery. Was there any hope of finding the portrait? And was it being taken care of properly, wherever it was?

Julie choked back a sob. "Lord, I don't understand this," she muttered. "Is this supposed to be some kind of experiment in faith? Does it have to be at such a price?"

With a sigh, and no answer to her questions, she pulled herself out of the chair and into some fresh clothes.

❧

When Julie returned to the dining room for breakfast, the meal had already begun.

"Aren't you excited?" Mary Ellen Ventura cooed. "This is your big day. I can't wait for tonight. I'm looking forward to it more than I can say."

Julie forced a smile. "Yes, we've been waiting a long time for this."

Lisa Butler slathered butter on a muffin. "Are you all right, Julie? You look beat."

"Yeah," Theo said. "What's wrong?"

"I didn't sleep much last night," Julie replied, pouring herself some black coffee. She could not bring herself to think about eating anything yet.

"Too excited?" Mary Ellen speculated. "I know I wouldn't sleep a wink if I were having an art show of my own. I can't even imagine how you must be feeling."

No, you can't, Julie thought silently. *Maybe there won't even be a show.* She settled into an empty chair at the end of the table, opposite Larry.

"Aw, Julie's going to be fine," Dayton Edwards declared. "I was down at the showroom yesterday, helping out. Everything is in tiptop shape."

Julie looked frantically to Larry for help. Should they explain to everyone what happened? After all, Dan Rakes had said that he wanted to interview all of them. Perhaps they should be warned. Even with her misgivings about Dayton Edwards, she could not imagine that any one of them was involved. But they should be prepared for the police to approach them.

As if reading her thoughts, Larry nodded ever so slightly.

"I was going to say something when everyone was together," Larry began. "Does anyone know if Mr. Lamp is coming down to breakfast?"

Della moved around the table, pouring orange juice. "He checked out about an hour ago. He said he did not even have time for breakfast."

Larry flinched almost imperceptibly. Julie's eyes widened at his alarm. Did he think Fenway Lamp had something to do with the theft?

"Wasn't his reservation through the weekend?" Larry asked his mother.

"You've forgotten that he said he was winding up his business late yesterday," Theo Butler said, pointing a playfully accusing finger at Larry.

How late? Julie asked herself silently. *Maybe about midnight?* Immediately she chastised herself for thinking Fenway Lamp had anything to do with the missing paintings. He was a quiet, hardworking man who flattered Leed House with his repeat business.

"Well, then, I guess we can get started," Larry said.

"Started with what, Paxton?" Dayton Edwards demanded. "What is going on around here?"

"The Flagg Gallery was robbed last night," Larry said simply.

Around the table jaws dropped.

"Oh no!" exclaimed Mary Ellen. "The paintings. . .are they . . .?"

"Three are missing," Julie said hoarsely.

"I'm so sorry to hear that," Lisa said sympathetically. "What a dreadful thing to happen on the day of the opening."

"First your car, now this," observed Dayton.

"What happened to her car?" Theo asked.

"Got hit yesterday," Dayton answered. "Hit-and-run. She can't drive it."

Mary Ellen gasped.

"It's okay," Julie said with a false sense of security. "The police are looking into everything. I don't really care about the car. But I would like to get the paintings back."

"Of course you would," Lisa said. "What about the show?"

Julie shrugged. "I'm not sure. I guess I'll talk to the police again this morning, or maybe try to get hold of David Flagg. Or Vanessa. I'm not sure what to do."

"We'll just do one thing at a time," Larry said softly. He turned to Dayton.

"Dayton, were you still at the showroom when the work was finished for the day?"

"Yeah. Why?"

"There seems to be some question whether the alarm system was functioning properly. Do you know if Vanessa activated it?"

Dayton cocked his head to think. "I remember she went around checking doors. But I don't know anything about an alarm system." He shrugged and reached for the muffin basket. "Guess I'm not too much help."

"She *always* sets the alarm," Julie insisted. "It if wasn't working, that's another question. But she never forgets to activate it."

Theo Butler set his fork down and looked thoughtful. "Maybe a customer? Someone who has seen your work but couldn't afford it?"

Julie shook her head and shrugged one shoulder. "My paintings are not expensive. There would be no reason to steal them. I'm an unknown in the art world."

"Maybe, but maybe not," Lisa said. "At least in Maine, people are starting to recognize your name."

"You think so?"

"Sure. I heard about you several months ago. I had no idea I would ever meet you, but a friend of mine was raving about a seascape you painted."

"I don't know what to think," Julie said weakly.

"What do you know about those guys Flagg hired to hang paintings?" Dayton asked.

"Not much," Julie said. "I'm pretty sure he has used the same guys before, though. Besides, I did not get the idea that they were art aficionados."

"Of course it's important to figure out who took the paintings," Larry mused. "But what is more mysterious is why."

"And why only three?" Dayton said. "A lot of those paintings are small enough to be carried off without too much trouble."

Julie and Larry had to agree with that.

Julie looked past Larry, through the doorway, and into the kitchen. Della was fidgeting around the stove, but Julie could tell she was not really doing anything. She wished Della would just come in and sit down with the guests, but she never did.

"I'm afraid I have to tell all of you that the police will probably want to question you today," Larry said.

"What for?" Lisa Butler asked.

"Are we suspects?" Mary Ellen Ventura asked dramatically, her eyes widening.

"Not exactly," Larry answered. "But you've all been around Seabridge for a few days now. Maybe you saw something or heard something and you don't realize it. I'm sure they just want to check out all the possibilities."

Julie appreciated Larry's effort to put the guests at ease, when in fact Officer Rakes did consider them all suspects, at least until he could eliminate them in a way that satisfied his standards. She knew he would be irritated that Fenway Lamp had slipped out of the noose and probably had left town already.

"I've never been questioned by the police before," Mary Ellen said. "I can't imagine that I have any useful information, but of course I want to cooperate."

"We all do, I'm sure," Dayton said.

Conversation lagged as everyone soaked up the impact of the information Larry had given. Della came in with more muffins and everyone concentrated on eating for a few minutes. Della retreated to the kitchen once again.

Larry broke the silence. "Hey, Dayton," Larry said lightheartedly, a distinct contrast in mood. "I was out for a walk this morning and I didn't see your car in the lot."

"My car? Oh, that was a rental. I decided I wasn't really using it very much and turned it in yesterday. I'm leaving tomorrow anyway. Or at least I was, until this mess happened."

"I didn't realize it was a rental. That was a pretty sporty looking set of wheels."

"Yeah, I got lucky. I had specifically requested an economy compact but they didn't have one. So they gave me that coupe for the budget rate."

"It was an unusual color. What do you suppose they call that at the factory? Was it metallic something or other?"

"Don't know. I just called it green."

Julie unconsciously held her breath through this interchange. Larry was making it sound as natural as possible, but he was definitely probing. Dayton's answers were cool and unruffled. He steadily shoveled double portions of food into his mouth as he had for the last four mornings. Julie did not know whether to be suspicious or not.

"Speaking of cars, what about yours?" Lisa asked. "Was the damage bad?"

Julie roused herself to answer the question. "The front end was smashed in so much that it had to be towed. But I think it will just be a matter of body work in that spot." She looked at Larry for corroboration.

"Yes, I think it looks worse than it is," Larry said. "The insurance company won't be too happy about it, but that's the way it goes."

Dayton pushed back from the table. "Well, since I'm obviously on foot today, I won't be going far. I have some errands, but I'll check back later and see if the police are coming around."

Julie nodded. "I don't think any of you need to feel housebound. If you could just let us know where to find you. . ."

"Of course," Theo said.

"I had planned to hike again today, but perhaps I'll just visit the shops," Mary Ellen said.

Julie was grateful when the guests had dispersed. She sat at one end of the long table, staring at Larry. At last Della came in and sat with them.

"Why didn't you come in earlier, Mom?" Larry asked.

"I couldn't stand the thought of looking my guests in the eye when one of them may be a criminal."

"Let's not jump to conclusions," Larry warned.

"But we can't be naive, either," Julie argued. She was determined not to make that mistake again. "I don't want to believe it either, but someone is trying to hurt me, and it might be someone right under our noses."

The phone rang in the hall.

ten

"That was Dan Rakes," Larry said, coming back from the hall after answering the phone.

Julie jerked her head toward Larry. "Did he find *Triumph*?"

"No, Sweetheart, I'm afraid not." Larry's voice was barely above a whisper.

Julie turned her face away, not wanting Larry to see the tears brimming in her eyes. She stared into the blackness in her coffee cup.

"What did he have to say?" Della asked. She started stacking breakfast dishes.

"He's going to interview our guests this morning. Then he has a few more questions for you, Julie."

"I don't know anything else to tell him," Julie moaned.

"He's just trying to be thorough. We have to let him do his job the best way he knows how."

Julie nodded, wordless.

"What about the show tonight?" Della asked practically.

"He's aware of it. If it is at all possible, he will have his people out of there by lunch time."

"What does he have to do?" In Julie's mind, the crime scene had not yielded much information. It seemed pointless for the police to linger.

"They just want to be sure any clues have been examined or removed before a crowd of people comes in and destroys something they need."

"Julie, maybe you should go down there," Della said. "You need to look after your paintings."

"I agree," Larry said quickly. "I'll take you down."

"I'll just be in the way," Julie protested. She was not sure she wanted to see those empty hooks again.

"You won't be in the way. You have a right to be there."

"But I don't really need to be there."

"We have to see if the show can open." Larry moved toward Julie and reached out to put a hand on her shoulder. "I know how grieved you are about *Triumph*. But the immediate question is whether to go forward with the show. What do you want to do?"

"I don't know what I think about anything right now." She laid her face against his hand and closed her eyes.

"We'll get hold of David and call the whole thing off if you want to."

Julie sat straight up and shook her head. "No, I can't do that. It wouldn't be fair to David. He's worked hard on this. He has more than earned any commission he might get. After all, I wasn't going to sell *Triumph* anyway, and the landscapes. . . well, they didn't mean as much to me."

"Nevertheless, I'm sure David would understand if you wanted to cancel. Maybe he would prefer to cancel, since his mother is sick."

"I don't know how to get hold of him in Vermont. He could be on his way back now."

"How about Vanessa?" Della said. "She told the police she was sick, but maybe she has heard from David."

Julie sighed. "I don't know. I guess we should go see what's happening."

"So we'll go," Larry said with finality.

"Did you eat anything yet?" Della asked sternly.

Julie shook her head. "My stomach's too jittery."

"You have to eat. It's going to be a long day."

"I don't think—"

Larry interrupted and reached into a basket on the table. "We'll take a muffin along. Maybe you'll feel like eating later."

"At least drink some juice," Della pleaded.

Julie obliged her with a thick swallow of orange juice.

❧

At the showroom, the scene had not changed from a few hours earlier. If not for the guard outside the door, an onlooker would never know that the building had been burglarized during the quiet night. It simply appeared that three of the paintings had not been hung yet. Julie blinked back tears and looked again at the spot where *Triumph* should have been. The portrait had been the focal point of the entire display. Now the silver hooks hung mute and empty. Julie envisioned her grandmother's face looking back at her from the wall, a face from ten years ago, before the illness had taken away her spark. *Oh, Grammy,* she thought to herself. *How could this happen?*

"What happened here? Why is there a police officer outside my door?" David Flagg's voice barraged the room.

Julie turned toward him with a mixture of relief and dread. "They tried to reach you last night," she started to explain, not knowing where to begin.

"What for?" he thundered.

Julie could hardly speak. "Someone stole some of the paintings."

David looked around, doing a quick mental inventory. "*Triumph* and two landscapes."

"Right."

David glanced back at the door. "How did they get in? The door doesn't look forced."

"The police don't think it was forced," Julie said.

"Then how did they get in?" David repeated.

"David," Larry said to his friend, "do you have any reason to think the security system was not working properly?"

"I checked it myself, day before yesterday. It was fine."

"It looks like it's been disarmed."

"Not by me, it hasn't." David remained agitated, but at least he had stopped shouting.

Larry shrugged. "Someone else, then."

"Who?" David demanded. "How?"

"That's what we'd all like to know."

"Where is Vanessa?"

"I was hoping she would be here," Julie said. "But she was sick last night."

"She was fine when I left yesterday."

"I know. But later—"

"She'd better have a good explanation for this." David's jaw was set emphatically.

"It's not her fault, David," Julie said, so calmly that she surprised herself. "You know how careful she always is."

"The verdict is not in on that yet," David growled. "I left her in charge when I left for Vermont."

"How is your mother?" Julie suddenly remembered why David had been gone.

"My mother is fine. Fit as a fiddle, except for her usual arthritis."

Julie stared at him, puzzled.

"That message was a bunch of gobbledygook," David said. Irritation waved across his face.

"What do you mean?" Larry asked.

"I mean my sister never sent me a fax and my mother most certainly did not have a stroke. I've been driving around New England for the last twenty-four hours for absolutely no reason."

Julie and Larry were speechless.

"Someone set this up," Larry said quietly and gloomily. He and Julie stared at each other as the truth set in.

"I want some answers, and I want them now!" David bellowed.

High heels clicked across the floor. The three of them turned their heads toward the sound.

"Want answers for what?" Vanessa asked.

David turned toward her. "Just where have you been?"

"Throwing up most of the night, if you must know," Vanessa said evenly. "If I could have come down earlier, I would have."

Julie silently inspected Vanni's face. It did look a little green and there were bags under her eyes.

"Are you feeling better now?" Julie asked, genuinely concerned for her friend but also searching for something believable.

"I feel like death warmed over," Vanni answered. "But at least I've stopped upchucking. Given the circumstances, I didn't think I had any choice but to come down here." She gestured over her shoulder. "This fellow Stubbs was watching my apartment all night anyway."

Stubbs was leaning against the door frame across the room. "We have a few questions for you," he said somberly.

Vanessa sighed heavily, looked around, and shuffled toward a folding chair. "I have to sit down." Even sick and sleepless, Vanessa was strikingly beautiful. Dressed as impeccably as ever in a navy linen suit, she drew her legs to one side in a feminine posture. Her dark hair cascaded perfectly around her shoulders.

Stubbs took out a small notebook and approached her. "Where were you between eleven and two o'clock last night?"

"You know very well I was in my apartment—sick!" she snapped.

"Can anyone verify that?"

"You can try asking my cat," she said dourly. "Otherwise I live alone. And I was alone last night."

Stubbs made some studious notes. "Did any neighbors see you come in. . .anything like that?"

Vanessa was exasperated and scowled at him. "I don't think so. I don't remember seeing anyone."

"No one on the stairs or in the hall?" Stubbs would not let up.

"Didn't I just say no?"

"What about you, Mr. Flagg?" Stubbs asked.

"What about me?"

"Where were you between eleven and two last night?"

"Catching some shut-eye on my sister's couch after going on a wild goose chase."

"Can your sister verify this?"

"Of course she can. You don't seriously think I set up the theft of my own gallery, do you?"

"Just asking questions."

"If these are the best questions you can think of, we'll never find those paintings."

Stubbs kept writing. Julie watched the interchange, intimidated and afraid to open her mouth.

The showroom door opened, and Dan Rakes entered. "I see the missing parties have been located," he said dryly.

"Rakes, what is going on here?" David demanded.

"I'm trying to find some paintings, David."

"Well, they aren't here."

Rakes glared at David. David glared back.

"Look, David, we're just trying to do our jobs. If your security system had been working, this might not be happening."

"My security system was working."

"Not according to the report I got."

David turned to Vanessa. "Well?"

"I set the alarm system when I left, just like I always do."

"My experts tell me that the system was properly disarmed," Dan said, "as if it had never been set."

David threw his hands up in frustration. "Look, Rakes, I don't have time to debate that right now. We're supposed to open an art show here in about seven hours."

"And I'm trying to get out of your way. We've dusted everything we can for prints. That's about all we have to go on right now."

"Well, then, get going."

Dan flipped his notebook shut. "Stubbs, I think we're finished here. Let's let these folks get back to business."

The police left. Julie, Larry, David, and Vanessa were left staring at each other. Weighty, unanswered questions hung between them.

David put his hands on his hips and asked. "Are we going to do this show or not?"

"Certainly!" said Vanessa. "You still want to, don't you, Julie?"

"Y-yes, I think so." She did not dare say no. Although she was spinning in confusion about the theft, standing there in the midst of all her work, she did want to continue.

"Look on the bright side," Vanni said. "The added publicity from the theft will be a great boost to the show. It may even jack up prices."

Julie stared at her, hardly believing Vanni could say something like that.

"There is no bright side to this," Larry chastised. "Julie has lost a painting she cares very much about. Even if everything else sells tonight, *Triumph* is still gone."

"Sorry," Vanessa mumbled, stepping back. "I was just trying to lighten things up." She turned and walked away without saying more.

Vanessa is acting even more strangely than yesterday, Julie thought. *Has the crisis brought on this behavior? Or her illness?*

"I'd better call the caterer," David said, getting back to business. "I'm not sure I trust her right now. It would be just like her to forget about us completely." He shuffled off, muttering to himself more than to anyone else.

Larry reached out and pulled Julie in for a hug. "This is really awful, Julie. There's nothing I can say to make it better. But I'm here. I'll stay with you all day. Just let me know what I can do for you."

"Thanks," she said into his shoulder. "I'm really exhausted. Maybe we could just go home and try to get some sleep."

&

Out in the street they were met by Charles Brooke, walking briskly toward them on the sidewalk.

"Julie, I just heard the news from Harold at the hardware store. Any progress?" Charles spoke in low, sympathetic tones and looked probingly into her eyes.

Julie shook her head. "I don't think they have any idea who did it," she said. "I sure don't." She looked in Charles's face, touched by his genuine concern.

"What about the driver of the car?" Charles asked.

"You mean the one who hit me?"

"Right. Maybe there's a connection."

"We've thought of that," Larry said.

"I've thought about it all night," Julie said. "I can't think of anyone who has a grudge against me. I think it's just coincidence."

"Maybe, maybe not," Charles said thoughtfully. He turned to Larry. "What did you find out about that fellow's car?"

"Dayton Edwards? He says that it was rented and that he

turned it in yesterday because he wasn't using it enough."

"Do you buy that?" Charles asked skeptically.

"I'm not sure. It's true that a lot of things are within walking distance of Leed House, but not everything. I use my car all the time."

"I think he had another reason for turning in the car."

"But if it was in an accident. . . ," Julie was putting the pieces together.

"It should be easy to find," Charles finished her thought. "There aren't that many places around here to rent a car from."

Larry shook his head. "No, he wouldn't be that foolish. He got rid of the car some other way."

"You think it wasn't rented at all, don't you?" asked Julie.

Larry nodded. "I think it was his own car and he put it someplace."

"If we can find it, we might be on to something," Charles said.

Julie shook her head insistently. "That still doesn't prove anything about last night. As far as we know, Dayton was at Leed House all night."

"As far as we know," Larry said. "But we can't be certain he was there the whole time. He's been with us long enough to know that there's a spare key for guests on the hook in the kitchen."

"I think we're jumping ahead of ourselves," Julie persisted.

"Maybe, maybe not," Charles said. "I'm going to have a talk with Officer Rakes. You just concentrate on the show tonight. I'll see you later."

Julie watched as Charles turned and strode up the street confidently as if he could take her problems on his shoulders and carry them away. Strangely, she did feel relieved. She almost smiled.

eleven

The autumn evening came gently. As the sun slithered behind the historic town square, it splashed a pinkish hue across the sky. In a matter of minutes, it faded into gray and dusk was full. A breeze stirred, rustling leaves and urging people to reach for their sweaters, another reminder that the long leisure days of summer were past for another year.

Light from the Flagg showroom down the street glowed softly with an inviting warmth. Adjacent shops were closing for the evening, but the art show was just beginning. Up and down the street, cars were parked and their passengers sauntered toward the showroom.

Inside, the atmosphere was festive, giving no hint of the crime that had occurred there less than twenty-four hours earlier. Despite David Flagg's anxiety, the caterer had arrived on time; a sumptuous display of finger food sprawled over four six-foot-long tables. Two women in black dresses and white chiffon aprons kept the serving dishes filled, while two young waiters with beverages circulated through the growing crowd. Tasteful classical music wafted through the air at just the right volume, loud enough to be enjoyed pleasantly but not so loud as to obscure conversation.

Julie stood to one side of the room, a plastic smile on her face. Her dress, a modest basic black gown, was fitted to the waist and fell softly around her calves. A lace bodice inset matched the lace sleeves that flowed generously and graciously from her shoulders. Her grandmother's pearls hung around her neck as if they were part of the dress. She had gone back to the hairdresser to have her hair freshly styled, and now she was almost afraid to turn her head too rapidly. Nervously she reached up with one hand to make sure the pearl earrings were still in place.

Julie looked over at Vanessa, who was daintily filling her plate at the serving table and urging guests of the show to do the same. Somehow Vanni's smile looked sincere. The stress of the day was not hindering her charm and gregariousness. Her gown was sophisticated, a deep teal satin, sleek against her slim form. Her hair hung in a wave around her shoulders and bounced freely and naturally as she laughed and conversed. This was the perfect environment for Vanessa Parker. She seemed completely at home. Julie could imagine that this is what Vanni was like when she made sales calls around the state: every hair in place, the perfect glint of pleasure in her eyes, thorough professional competence.

Julie, on the other hand, was a ball of nerves. David had encouraged her to stand near the door and let people know who she was as soon as they entered. But after stumbling over her words three times in a row and hardly being able to say good evening without stuttering, she had moved away from the door a few feet, then a few feet more. Her throat was parched, but she was too nervous to go to the refreshment table or to catch the eye of a waiter. If someone spoke to her, she would have to talk, but her tongue was too twisted up for that right now.

"You look lonely over here."

She turned to her right toward the sound of the voice and was relieved to see Larry approaching with a glass of punch in his hand.

"Thirsty?" he asked.

"Thank you." Gratefully, she drained the punch glass.

"You look a little pale," Larry said. "Are you sure you're

all right?"

"No, I'm not sure. I'm incredibly nervous."

He put an arm across the back of her shoulders. "Relax. This is your big night."

"That's exactly why I can't relax. What if nobody likes my work?"

Larry gestured around the room with his free arm. "How can you even think that? Look around you. Everybody is having a great time."

"They're just being polite."

"Don't be ridiculous. People are really enjoying the show, and I'm sure you'll sell some paintings."

"I hope so. I'm afraid if David doesn't make enough money off of this, he'll drop me completely."

"I don't think you have anything to worry about."

Julie sighed. "I wish I could be that confident."

"It's a mystery to me why you doubt yourself so much," Larry said. "You've been building up a good track record for the last year and a half. David and Vanessa have both been successful with your paintings. What will it take to make you believe in yourself?"

"Uh-oh," Julie said. "Here comes Sharon Jennings. I just know I'm going to get tongue-tied again."

"You'll be fine," Larry said encouragingly.

"Julie," Sharon said, "what a wonderful show. And such a nice turnout."

"Yes, everyone has been so kind," Julie answered. She concentrated as fiercely as she could on this bit of small talk.

"Such a lovely atmosphere," Sharon said. "The food is great . . .and the music!"

"The credit for all that goes to David and Vanessa."

"They sure know what they're doing." Then Sharon wandered away.

"See," Larry whispered into her ear. "That wasn't so bad."

Theo and Lisa Butler suddenly appeared in front of Julie, their plates full from the food tables.

"This is really delightful," Lisa said, popping a black olive in her mouth. "I'm glad we stayed the extra day."

"Delightful and expensive," Theo added. "I think she's got her eye on something."

Lisa poked him with her elbow. "If you want a good price, you have to be more subtle than that."

Julie laughed. "I have been given strict instructions not to get involved in discussions about prices. I'm afraid you'll have to dicker with David Flagg."

"I was afraid of that. He looks tough."

"He's a businessman, that's for sure."

"Lisa has been known to drive a hard bargain, too," Theo said. "If anybody can talk him down, she can."

"Oh, look," Larry said. "Here comes Aunt Joanna."

"I can't believe she came out for this," Julie said, turning to watch her grandmother's childhood friend come through the door. Lisa and Theo watched with curiosity as a small, frail, bent woman leaned on the arm of a companion in her thirties. Together they took small steps across the floor.

"Who is Aunt Joanna?" Lisa asked. "Is she really your aunt?"

"Everyone calls her that," Larry explained.

"She looks ancient," Theo said.

"She is," Julie explained. "She's ninety-six. She and my grandmother grew up together. She married right out of high school and never left Seabridge."

"She knew your grandmother? It's neat to have her here."

"It's the next best thing to having my grandmother here."

Julie's eyes went to the spot where the painting of her grandmother should have been hanging. David had decided to leave the spot empty. Perhaps letting people know of the theft would spark someone's memory.

"Excuse me," Julie said, and moved toward Aunt Joanna.

"Julie, dear," Aunt Joanna said, grasping her arm. "So now you are a famous artist."

Julie laughed. "Not quite, Aunt Joanna. Thank you for coming. I didn't expect to see you."

"When I found out my granddaughter was coming, I insisted she bring me."

"I'm glad you did. There's plenty to eat. I hope you enjoy yourself."

"Wouldn't your grandmother be proud now," Aunt Joanna commented. "And she would laugh to see that your success came right here in Seabridge. She always thought she had to get away from here."

"Well, I'm so glad *you're* here. Look around, but let me know if you have any questions."

Aunt Joanna shuffled off on the arm of her granddaughter, as Julie looked on and smiled.

Julie's eyes went to David Flagg, standing erect in a tuxedo and looking the part of a distinguished businessman. His eyes were alert to observe anyone who lingered more than usual over a particular painting. She watched as he gradually made his way across the room and struck up a conversation with a young woman who had been standing for a long time in front of a winter landscape.

Vanessa kept people eating and enjoying themselves. At one point she cocked her ear to listen to the music, realized it was finishing, and went to put on a fresh stack of compact discs. She was swift and efficient, with a flashing smile for everyone. Julie watched her smooth movements, amazed that Vanessa seemed so unaffected by the events of the night before. The theft was never out of Julie's mind.

"Oh, Julie, there you are."

Julie turned to see Mary Ellen Ventura gushing toward her.

"I just love your paintings," Mary Ellen said. "They're absolutely gorgeous."

"Thank you." In only a few days, Julie had come to know Mary Ellen well enough to give only simple responses. No doubt Mary Ellen would carry the conversation.

"I do wish I could buy a painting and take it back to Iowa with me. I've tried to be frugal during this trip, but I know I can't possibly pay what such beautiful paintings are worth."

"Maybe one of the smaller ones," Larry said as he took up his place beside Julie again. "Or a framed sketch."

"Maybe so. I shall have to talk to Mr. Flagg, I suppose. I'm not very good at negotiating. But I would like one of the paintings." She glanced around the room. "Has Dayton arrived yet?"

"Dayton?" Julie asked.

"Yes, he was planning to come, I'm certain of it. I talked with him this afternoon. And I know he would give anything to have that picture of the yard behind Leed House. I heard him talking about it a few days ago."

"Oh?" Julie said, suddenly interested in what Mary Ellen was saying. "Who was he talking to?"

"I don't know," Mary Ellen answered, waving her hand airily. "He was talking on the phone in the hall, telling someone about it."

Julie's eyes met Larry's.

"So you haven't seen him?" Mary Ellen asked again.

"No, we haven't see him yet tonight," Larry said.

"I guess I'd better get my bid in on something before everything I can afford is snatched up." Mary Ellen trailed away.

"What do you suppose she meant by all that?" Julie asked.

"Coming from her, I'm sure it's just innocent chatter," Larry answered.

"Do you suppose she knows something about Dayton we don't know?"

"I doubt it. Probably she told us everything she knows."

"Or everything that she remembers at the moment."

"She's right; he said more than once that he was coming. I'm sure he'll turn up."

"Considering the effort he put into helping set things up, it is strange that he's not here already."

"Look, here comes Charles."

Julie looked up just in time to see Charles rush toward her enthusiastically and plant a kiss on her cheek. She felt her face blush and looked nervously at Larry, who seemed amused.

"How is the artist tonight?" Charles said. He squeezed her hand and held on to it.

"She's a little nervous," Larry answered.

"More than a little," Julie clarified.

"I know what happened earlier in the day clouds things tonight, but it's still a great night for you."

"Yes," she agreed. "I can't believe so many people have come out."

"And tomorrow there will be more."

"I can't imagine that." She was aware that he was still holding her hand. She glanced at Larry again.

"Just wait. Tomorrow will be great." Charles turned to Larry. "Can I chat with you for a moment?"

"Sure. Let's step away from the spotlight here and let Julie continue to greet her royal subjects."

"No, that's all right—" Julie protested, but they had already moved away from her, their heads huddled together.

Julie strained to hear what they were saying to each other, but she could not make out anything. She could see Charles was talking and Larry was listening intently. Charles gestured as he spoke, but even that did not give her any clues about what he was saying. Worry lines appeared in Larry's forehead. Just when she had decided to interrupt them and demand to be included, Della caught Julie's arm.

"David has done a wonderful job," Della oozed. "I've heard so many people saying how lovely your paintings are."

Julie let her shoulders sag in the safety of Della's company. "I'm so nervous! But everything seems to be going well."

"Vanessa is looking great, her usual charming self. Oh, here she comes."

"Hey kiddo!" Vanessa said enthusiastically. "You're doing great here tonight."

"Thanks, but you're the one who put this all together."

"Don't be modest. There would have been no reason for the show if it hadn't been for your paintings."

Julie smiled politely but nervously. "You look like you're feeling better," she observed.

"Absolutely. Must have been some twenty-four-hour bug. I feel great now."

Julie nodded. *Yes, of course, a twenty-four-hour bug.* Still, it seemed strange that no one who had worked with Vanni in the last few days had gotten sick. With a sigh, she shook the thought out of her mind.

"Dare I ask. . .?" Julie started hesitantly.

"About sales?" Vanni tilted her head thoughtfully, bouncing her wavy hair. "It's a little too soon to predict, but I'd say we're doing well for this early in the show."

"That's reassuring." Julie pivoted her head to scan the room. "I thought Dayton Edwards would be here tonight. He put in a lot of work here yesterday."

Vanni looked puzzled. "I don't know what happened to him. Maybe some business came up."

Somehow Julie doubted that.

"Gotta scoot. I think we have a hot prospect for the back view of Leed House."

Vanessa glided away. Larry reappeared at Julie's side.

"What happened to Charles?" Julie asked.

"He couldn't stay. Said he'd come back tomorrow when he could stay longer."

"What did he want?"

Larry shrugged. "Oh, just had some questions."

Julie looked into Larry's eyes. He managed to meet her gaze, but she suspected he was not telling her everything.

"Forget it, Julie. It was nothing. Let's go get something to eat."

Julie was suddenly aware of an insidious headache and agreed that eating was a good idea. Meekly, she followed Larry to the serving table.

twelve

The tray rattled as the waiter let it drop to the table; then he slumped into a chair behind the food table. Clearly he did not want another person to come looking for food. There was not much food left to be had. . .a stray black olive, some soggy finger sandwiches, a few broken gourmet cookies. Not much else. The punch bowl was empty and there seemed to be no need to fill it again.

The party was over. The weekend show would close in a matter of minutes.

Julie watched as the worn out young man leaned his head back against the wall and let his eyes close for just a minute. He had worked Friday evening and all day Saturday and Sunday. He had been there as much as she had. If he was half as tired as she was, then she was glad to extend her silent sympathy. In fact, all of the caterer's help looked exhausted.

Automatically, Julie reached out to shake the hand of a departing guest, smiled, and said, "Thanks so much for coming." She had gotten over her nervousness of opening night and was now on autopilot. Only a handful of diehard viewers remained in the showroom at nine o'clock on Sunday night. Julie decided to wait them out in a more comfortable position. Her grateful eyes settled on a padded folding chair parked against the wall. The hem of her calf-length pleated white wool skirt brushed the floor as she sat down. Though glad to be sitting, she forced herself to maintain a smile and an erect posture. The shoulder pads in her matching sweater helped to maintain the image, making it appear more effortless than it was.

From this perspective, Julie could scan the entire room. The view was peppered with little orange "sold" tags hanging from frames, each spot of color a reassurance that she had done well with the show. She no longer worried about whether David would make any money from her work. Clearly he had, and so had she. Julie was a bit nervous about finding out exactly how much.

The three days of the show were a blur. Later, she would study the guest book to discover just who had been there. Many were tourist browsers and others were townspeople ready to cheer her on. But a fair number had seemed to be serious art collectors who were relying on the reputation of the Flagg Gallery to make their visit worthwhile.

Dayton Edwards had breezed in during the afternoon of the second day, but he had not stayed long and had not purchased a painting. Julie thought it strange that he did not even comment on the fact that the painting he had been considering was already sold by the time he got there. He had just flashed his charming smile, kissed her cheek like they were old friends, and then went on his way. Later she found out he had checked out of Leed House shortly after his visit to the gallery.

Charles had stopped in each of the three days of the show, looking carefully at all the paintings and dropping hints for the painting he hoped she would create for the church. She found she enjoyed having him around, just to talk to and nibble with. Charles also had repeated conversations with Larry, who came and went as his schedule demanded. To Julie, it was odd to be receiving so much attention from both of them, but also reassuring to have them around.

Occasionally, curiosity about what Larry and Charles were conspiring crossed Julie's mind, but never at a moment when she was free to act on her impulse and pursue an explanation.

As the hours of the show passed, the urgency of finding out what they were up to waned. Julie was fully involved with her own audience and prospective customers who wanted to understand the inspiration behind certain paintings. She did not have time to wonder about many things unrelated to the show.

Julie realized she had let herself sink back against the chair for support. Then she heard the showroom door creak open and shut and knew that she had been daydreaming and had missed the last of the guests. Looking a bit haggard, David locked the door behind the departing pair and hung up the closed sign. He leaned against the door with satisfaction.

"Well, Julie, you did it. I'd say that was a fine show, for the first time out."

"I owe it all to you," Julie said.

"Let's not go down that lane again," David said, waving away her sentiment. "Now we've got to take this show apart. We've still got work to do."

"I'll say we have!" Vanessa joined the conversation enthusiastically. "It'll take us all night to add up the profits."

Larry joined the trio and reached out to pull Julie to her feet.

"I can't believe you're still here," Julie said, accepting his light kiss. "You didn't have to stay to the bitter end."

"The end doesn't sound so bitter to me," Larry bantered. "This is the really good part."

The waiters slung their jackets over their shoulders and gestured that they were leaving. The women serving the food were right behind them, with the assurance that they would all be back in the morning to clean up.

"What needs to be done tonight, David?" Larry asked.

"Not too much. We can all go home and get some rest and deal with this tomorrow."

"Are you sure?" Larry asked. "I don't mind staying for a while."

"Me neither," Julie said. "I don't think I could sleep now anyway."

David looked around. "Well, Julie can take a look at what is left and decide what she wants me to try to sell in the shop and what she wants to keep."

"Well, there are a few I might take back," Julie admitted.

"If you're up to it, you could take them tonight. That way they won't get lost in the shuffle tomorrow when we try to put everything back to normal."

"There's a box and some packing paper in the back of the shop," Vanessa offered. "It's right on your desk. I'll get it for you."

"No, that's all right," Julie said. "You stick to the finances. Finding a cardboard box is more my speed."

"I'll go with you," Larry offered.

"That's not really necessary." She touched his arm lightly. "I'll be right back. Just relax for a moment."

"You sure?"

"Of course. I'll be just a minute."

As she crossed the gallery and slipped into the shop, Julie was aware of how much her feet hurt. She had been standing continuously for more than two days and wearing dress shoes that she was not used to. She longed to take off her shoes and rub her feet.

She walked through the dimly lit shop and found the box just where Vanessa had said it would be, on the little desk that Julie sometimes used in the back of the store. It held plenty of packing paper she could use to cushion several paintings transported in one box. She picked it up.

Immediately, Julie set the box down again. Alone in the dark, she had the perfect chance to pamper her feet for minute. She sat down in the swivel desk chair and gave a sigh as she slipped off her shoes. Wriggling her toes, she felt better already. Removing her shoes was risky because her feet might feel even worse when she had to put the shoes back on but, for the moment, freedom from heels was a delightful sensation.

The shop had a strange peacefulness about it, or perhaps it seemed that way because Julie had not had a moment to herself for at least four days. And they had not been ordinary four days, but time when she craved a few minutes to think. Her mind whirred with people and paintings and the strange thoughts that came from lack of sleep. Going from the theft straight into the show had demanded as much fortitude as she could muster and had left her with no time to think through things. She had not touched her sketch pad in four days, depriving herself of her usual method of exploring and expressing her emotions. Julie was anxious to restore normalcy to her life, although the mystery of the stolen paintings would haunt her until it was solved and that might be a very long time.

Julie was tempted to sit a few more minutes and relish the solitude, but she knew Larry was waiting for her. Reluctantly, she leaned down to find her shoes in the dark. She stopped in midmotion, sure that she had heard a sound that was not the familiar creak of her chair. It was more like a scuffing or shuffling.

"Larry?" she said aloud but tenuously. She did not really think it was Larry. The sound had come from the back of the shop, not from the gallery. As quietly as she could, and with a grimace, she stuffed her feet back into their painful prisons and sat up straight. She remained motionless for at least two minutes, hearing nothing. Finally she began to wonder if she had imagined the whole thing. She stood up, her hand on the cardboard box, ready to go. Then she heard it again.

She glanced toward the door from the gallery, where a thin stream of light filtered into the shop. David, Larry, and Vanessa were still there. Perhaps she should go get them. On the other hand, perhaps all she was hearing was a mouse trapped behind a piece of furniture. She decided against going for help and quietly stepped toward the back of the shop. She stopped when she stood outside the door to the storeroom. Once again she stayed perfectly still for what seemed like an eternity.

On impulse, she threw open the storeroom door to investigate for herself. As she expected, the door was not locked and it swung open easily. Inside, it was very dark. As she waited for her eyes to adjust, she groped along the wall with one hand, looking for the light switch. She never could remember where it was. Then she remembered it was ridiculously placed behind the door. To reach it, she would have to close the door. Stealthily, she stepped far enough into the room to close the door and reach for the switch.

Her fingers had not quite reached the switch when she heard the scuffing sound again. It was no mouse. Somebody was in that storeroom!

She drew her hand back from the light switch, wheeled around, and peered into the darkness.

"Who's in here?" she asked aloud. . .and instantly regretted giving away her location in the dark. The scuffing turned to a creak, and the gray shades in the shadows shifted. Movement! She was definitely not alone! Julie covered her mouth with her hands to keep from crying out again. Whoever was in the storeroom had just slipped across the room, behind a tall, gray, heavy shelving unit that held paint cans and assorted fixtures that David used in the shop.

Julie darted through the darkness toward the door, holding her breath and grasping for the door knob. But she was not fast enough. She heard a groan just before the heavy metal gray shelf toppled toward her. With the door still closed, she had no exit. She squeezed her eyes shut and raised her arms in vain defense. A paint can struck her torso and a corner of the shelf cut into her cheek as the falling unit pushed her to the floor. Her head cracked against the concrete. After that she blacked out.

thirteen

A hammer slammed against the inside of her skull, pounding, pounding. She wanted to cry out in pain but she could not find her voice. And from deep in the black hole, no one would hear her.

Then she heard voices. They were saying something familiar, but she was not quite sure of the words. Earnestly, they repeated themselves until their sounds echoed almost unbearably around her head.

"Julie! Can you hear me?"

"Wake up, Julie. Come on, open your eyes."

She came out of the groggy grayness slowly. The shapes hovering over her were indistinct, hardly more than shadows.

"That's it, Julie. Look at me. Can you see me now?"

Once again she tried to cry out. Her eyelids fell closed and she struggled to open them again.

"Did you call the ambulance?"

"The paramedics are on the way."

"What's taking so long?"

"They'll be here."

"Julie, try to wake up. I'm here, I'm right here."

Larry. The voice was Larry's. Julie felt his cool hand against her cheek. She blinked several times until at last her eyes focused. Swallowing heavily, she prepared to talk.

"Larry. . .I heard. . ."

"Take it easy. Don't try to talk. Just look at me. Try to focus your eyes."

Pain ripped through her face as she turned her head toward

his voice. Instinctively she raised her hand to her face and the pain tore a path through her shoulder.

"Don't move. Just lie still."

A different voice. Vanessa.

Julie swallowed again. Her vision was clearer now. She saw David, Vanessa, and Larry crouched around her, their faces hovering over hers. She watched as Larry whipped off his suit jacket, rolled it into ball, and gently positioned it under her head. That felt better.

"Somebody was here," Julie mumbled.

"Shhh," Larry said.

But Julie persisted. "There was somebody in here. I heard noises."

"Julie," said Vanessa softly, "maybe you shouldn't try to talk right now."

"But someone was here. Maybe they still are."

Larry looked at David. "She may have a point. Did either of you see anything? Or hear anyone go out?"

Vanessa shrugged. "All I heard was the crash. After that, I didn't really listen for any other noises."

David shook his head. "I'm sure whoever was here is long gone. We weren't paying any attention. But I'll go have a look around."

"Someone could easily have gone out the back door in the time it took us to get here from the showroom," Vanni said.

"I agree," Larry said. He turned back to Julie. "I don't think anyone is here, Julie, but David is checking."

"Be careful," Julie said feebly. If only she had been a little more careful herself. What had ever made her think she should go into the storeroom alone?

Slowly, she turned her head from side to side and surveyed the rubble around her. The metal shelf that had forced her to the floor was beside her, its contents scattered around the room. Her head and side pulsed with pain, reminding her of her foolishness and that she could have been hurt very badly or killed. Whoever had been in the storeroom had been up to no good. Was it the thief, coming back to steal more paintings? Dayton Edwards's image floated in her mind; his brief appearance at the show had been puzzling. The siren outside halted her thoughts. The ambulance had come.

⋆

Seabridge was too small for a hospital of its own. The closest one was twenty minutes away. Julie had protested being taken there. But her head was bleeding and her side screamed with pain; she had no real grounds to resist. The doctor in the emergency room patched her face, X-rayed her ribs, and ordered her to lie still while he went to look at the film.

Larry had come with her to the hospital. When they were alone, she turned to him. "Where are David and Vanessa? Are they coming here?"

"They wanted to, but the police had some questions."

"But they let you come with me."

"I didn't give them much choice," Larry said, squeezing her hand. "I wasn't going to let you be carried off to the hospital and not be with you."

Julie smiled weakly. "Thanks."

"I called Mom while you were being X-rayed."

"She'll be really upset."

"She was worried about you, of course. But she kept a level head. She's coming down."

"She doesn't have to do that."

"She loves you, Julie," Larry said simply. "We both do."

Julie heard his words but did not have the strength to contemplate their significance.

The curtain around the examining room parted. "Hi there," a voice said.

"Charles!" Julie said. "How did you—"

"Della called me," Charles explained, stepping up to the

side of her bed. "We came together, but they won't let her back here."

"How did you get in?"

"Clergy status." Charles grinned at his special privilege and pointed to his badge. "Comes in handy sometimes."

Julie managed a feeble laugh.

Larry rested a hand on Charles's shoulder. "Now that you're here, Charles, I'll go check with Mom," Larry said. He leaned over and gently kissed Julie's forehead. "I'll be right back. Maybe I can talk them into letting Mom come back here."

"Try hard," Julie said.

Charles settled onto a stool next to the bed. "Do you need to rest, Julie? I can just sit here quietly until Larry gets back." He looked at her softly.

"No, it's okay. My head's a lot clearer now than it was a while ago."

"What happened? Larry just told Della that they found you hurt in the storeroom."

"That's really all he knows. I heard something, a noise in the storeroom, and I went in to check on it."

"Alone?"

"I know. It was stupid. But I thought it was probably my imagination or maybe a mouse. And if it was something real, it would be gone by the time I got back with help."

"I suppose there is some logic in that. But with everything that has happened in the last few days. . ."

"I know. It was not one of the brightest things I've ever done."

"Did you see anything?"

"Just shadows, mostly. But it was a man, I'm sure of it. I could hear him breathing."

"Could you identify him?"

She shook her head, regretfully. "No. I didn't get a good look."

"Could it have been Dayton Edwards?"

Julie thought before answering. "I suppose it could have been. But I couldn't be sure." She turned her head to catch his eye. "Do you have reason to think it was Dayton? Do you know something I don't know?"

"Nothing specific. It's just that he was behaving so strangely yesterday."

"None of us really know him. Maybe that was normal for him."

"You have a point. . ." His voice drifted off.

"You know something, don't you?" Julie asked. "You were talking with Larry about something all during the show. What's going on?" She tried to push herself up on one elbow but immediately winced in pain.

"Take it easy, Julie."

"Tell me what's going on," she demanded, ignoring her agony.

"I will," Charles said. "But lie back. I doubt that you're supposed to be moving around like that."

"She certainly should not." The stern tone came from the doctor, returned with her X-rays.

Charles extended his hand. "Charles Brooke, pastor of the community church in Seabridge."

"Nice to meet you."

"How is she?" Charles gestured toward the oversized film in the doctor's hand.

"I'm afraid your parishoner has a cracked rib on the left side."

"She'll need a cast, then?"

"We can't really put a cast on it, but we'll have to be sure the area is immobilized," the doctor answered. He turned to Julie. "You'll have to keep still. I want you to stay in bed for a few days."

"But I can go home tonight?"

"I see no reason you need to stay in the hospital. Just lie still. I'll be back in a few minutes and we'll get you all set."

As the doctor left, a quick sob escaped Julie's throat. "Why is all this happening, Charles?"

He reached out and took her hand. Squeezing sympathetically, he said, "A lot has happened to you in the past few days, both good and bad."

"The bad outweighs the good, I think."

"Weren't you pleased with the show?"

"Yes, I suppose. But if I hadn't been involved with the show, the paintings would not have been stolen, and I would not have been poking around a storeroom by myself."

"I see your point. But you could not have known that any of this would happen."

"I suppose not," Julie muttered, still not satisfied. "I suppose now you'll say something about having faith in the hard times."

"Not if you don't want me to."

"Is this what faith is always like?"

"What do you mean?"

"It feels heavy. And dark."

"Are you sure that's faith you are describing?"

Julie looked at him, puzzled.

"It sounds more like doubt to me, or unfaith."

"I don't like the way it feels," Julie said plaintively. "But I can't help it."

"Your reaction is normal and understandable," Charles assured her. "But don't stop there. Think about your paintings, Julie. Any one of them. Do you see the light that you put into them? Deep down, I think that is how you are describing faith . . .with light."

"What does that have to do with what happened tonight? I'm lying here on a hospital bed with a cracked rib and a headache to beat all headaches."

"Hang onto your feelings. In a couple of days, when you can sit up more comfortably, I want you to sketch what you're feeling now."

"I don't get it, Charles."

"Just humor me, okay? Start thinking about how you would draw what you're feeling now."

"It would be dark."

"Probably," he agreed, "but not completely. Not just a blotch of black."

As she nodded her confused agreement, Julie remembered what they had been talking about before the doctor had returned.

"You were going to tell me something about Dayton Edwards," she said.

"I was?"

"Yes. I want to know what's going on. All this stuff is happening to me, you know. You and Larry can't go around like it's some mystery novel you're trying to solve."

"Is that what you think?" Charles was amused.

Julie was irritated. "Don't you laugh at me! Just tell me what's going on."

Charles shrugged. "Not much, really. I tried to track down Dayton's story about the car being a rental that he returned the day after the accident."

"Do you seriously think he's the one who hit my car?"

"Not anymore. Turns out his story is completely true. He did have a green rental car. But he turned it in, and there wasn't a scratch on it."

Julie sighed, painfully. "Then that doesn't mean anything, does it?"

"I told you there wasn't much to tell."

"Then why do I feel like you're holding something back?"

"Julie, there's nothing—"

Charles was interrupted by the return of Larry, with Della

in tow.

Julie raised her face slightly to receive Della's kiss on the cheek. "I thought they wouldn't let you back here! Did you sneak past the desk?"

Larry laughed. "No, we just nagged our way in."

"Are they going to move you to a room?" Della asked anxiously.

"No. I get to go home tonight."

"Are you sure that's wise? Forgive me for saying so, but you look terrible. I'm sure you'd be much better off if you just took a few days to rest and let the people here look after you properly. What if there is an injury they haven't found yet? Who's your doctor? I'll talk—"

"Mom," Larry said simply and quietly.

"I'm overreacting?" she asked.

He nodded.

Julie was smiling. "You're a sight for sore eyes. But I want to come home. The doctor says there's no need for me to stay, once he patches me back together."

"Cracked rib," Charles explained. "But she'll be just fine."

Della had moved into her next phase. "Well, I won't be having you climbing all those stairs to the tower. I'll fix you a bed on the ground floor where I can look after you properly."

"That's exactly what I need," Julie said.

Footsteps approached and the doctor appeared with a nurse. He scowled over the top of his glasses at the three visitors. "I don't recall calling a convention in this examining room. This is an emergency facility."

"And we were just leaving," Larry said, putting his hands on his mother's shoulders to steer her out. "Let us know when she's ready to go and we'll take her home."

fourteen

Leed House was quiet on Tuesday afternoon. The weekend guests had gone and no one new was expected until Thursday afternoon. The stately house with its enormous rooms was tranquil and settled. Della Paxton puttered around making sure everything was in its place, meticulously preparing for the next round of guests.

Julie sprawled comfortably on the sofa in the spacious parlor with a book in her lap. Under Della's watchful eye, she had hardly dared to move all day. Staring earnestly at the pages, she turned them at appropriate intervals, but her thoughts were elsewhere.

Officer Dan Rakes had dropped by earlier in the day to report on his investigation.

"What did the lab report say?" Larry had asked.

"Not much," Dan said. "They didn't find any prints."

"Not even on the shelves?" Julie questioned, surprised and disappointed by the news. "Those shelves are heavy. It was no accident that they got knocked over. Whoever was in there must have used both hands to push the shelves over."

"No doubt about it. But he also wore gloves. He was very careful."

Julie turned away, disheartened.

"What about all the prints you lifted from the main showroom?" Larry asked.

Dan shook his head. "Nothing. Zip. Everything we got was accounted for by people who had legitimate access to that room."

"But doesn't that narrow down your list of suspects? Somebody with legitimate access could have tampered with the alarm."

Dan was shaking his head. "Nope. We questioned everybody. Didn't come up with anything even remotely suspicious."

"There has to be something!" Julie cried out, and then winced with pain because she had tried to move too quickly.

"I'm sorry, but we had no legal grounds to hold anybody."

"What about Dayton Edwards?" Larry asked.

"What about him?" Dan countered. "He accounted for his whereabouts for the entire night of the theft. He was seen having dinner in a restaurant in town, then saw a movie. Your own mother verified that she locked up after he came in at eleven-fifteen that night."

"What about on closing night? He checked out of here, but do we really know where he went?"

"He took a bus over to Burton, then caught a train headed for Boston." Dan was one step ahead of Larry.

"I still don't trust him." Larry picked up a throw pillow and tossed it into a chair across the room. "My gut tells me he was not being completely honest with us while he was here."

"I understand. But it's not a crime to be untrustworthy. I can't press charges based on the feeling you have in your gut."

"I want my paintings back!" Julie said forcefully.

Dan Rakes remained calm. "Of course you do. And it's my job to find them. I'm doing everything I can."

"In the meantime I'm afraid to leave the house."

"Don't take the incident in the storeroom personally. It would have happened to anyone who opened the door just then."

Julie lifted a hand to her side. "Don't take it personally? Is that supposed to make me feel better?"

Dan shrugged. "I'm sorry you got hurt. And I'm sorry about the missing paintings. Give us some time."

"You've had five days already," Larry said. "The trail is getting cold."

"There you go again, sounding like a cheap detective novel."

"Sorry," Larry muttered.

"I'll get back to you as soon as I know something." Dan left then, leaving Julie and Larry staring hopelessly at each other.

Alone now, Julie shifted her position on the couch and mindlessly turned another page of the book. She was frustrated beyond words and she trembled with aggravation. Her first solo showing should have been a brilliant highlight of her career as an artist. Vanessa and David had no question that it had been a success from a business point of view. Yet the whole experience was wrapped in disappointment and was now shrouded in danger. And there was nothing she could do, nothing except try to stay out of the way of the next attack.

Setting aside her book, she picked up her sketch pad. Repeatedly she had tried to sketch. She was not being particular about results. She would draw anything at all. Wrapping her fingers around the pencil, she touched the tip to the paper and tried an experimental stroke. Free sketching, as she called it, was a device she often used to get her creativity flowing when she felt the urge to draw but could not focus on a subject. She stroked the page in several places, waiting for the familiar comforting surge of inspiration. It did not come. What she looked at now was not really a sketch, but just more doodling, some shapes placed on the page in a balanced but empty way. Most unsatisfactory. She flipped the pages of the sketch pad and examined her efforts of the last two days.

Julie had begun to think about creating another portrait of

her grandmother. *Triumph* could not be re-created, but she could highlight another dimension of her grandmother's strength, perhaps her faith. Grammy had always seemed to believe in something. In the drawing, a young Grammy reached toward a door. Julie was not sure why she had drawn that image, or why she had chosen to draw Grammy as a young woman. But it was definitely her grandmother's face, so much like her own, that was trapped on the page. But the sketch was weak. It had no power, no promise, as most of her sketches did. Was her talent being crippled by the events of the last few days? Would she be able to get past all this and create freely again?

"Tea time!" Della's cheery voice ruptured Julie's musings and she turned to smile at her friend.

"Thanks," Julie said. "I could use a pick-me-up."

"It's got lots of honey in it, just the way you like it," Della said, as she poured from the pot into two mugs.

"You pamper me too much," Julie said. "But, of course, I've told you that before and it never stops you."

"And it never will," Della declared solidly. "You've got a broken rib—"

"Just cracked," Julie corrected.

"Whatever. The point is you've been hurt and you need time to mend. So I'm here to make sure you do."

"You've been great. You and Larry both are taking such good care of me."

"Speaking of Larry, where has he gone?"

"Into town," Julie said. "He said he needed to go to the bank."

"That's odd. I just went yesterday and we haven't taken in any more money."

"Maybe he wants to take some out," Julie quipped.

"Whatever he's doing, I'm sure he has a good reason then."

Della leaned back in her chair and sipped her tea. "He would certainly never deceive you. He cares too much for you to trifle with you."

"I care about him, too," Julie said simply, unsure where Della was headed with this abrupt shift in the conversation.

"He was so proud of your art show, it was almost as if he deserved the credit himself. He was practically bursting with pride." Della propped her feet up on the coffee table and settled in for a talk. "I haven't seem him so excited in years."

"He seemed so calm to me. I guess I was too nervous most of the time to realize what was going on."

"He wanted to support you however he could. He would hush me if he heard me say this, but it's delightful to see him in love. I think this might be the real thing."

"The real thing?" Julie was starting to get uncomfortable. As close as she and Della were, she was not accustomed to discussing her relationship with Larry with his mother.

"Sure. I think he's going to propose soon."

Julie felt the color drain from her face. "He never. . .I mean, we. . ."

"Don't tell me you can't see it coming."

"Well, I. . .I don't know. . .I guess I haven't. . ."

"You've been working so long on your show. It's taken a lot of your energy. Larry would never want to get in the way of that. But that's over now. You won't be so busy for a while. I'm sure David and Vanessa will want you to keep painting and, before long, there will be another show. But somewhere in the middle of all this, you have to make room for a personal life. And Larry's ready."

"Ready?"

"To settle down. He's almost thirty, you know."

Much to Julie's relief, the phone rang and Della got up to answer it.

Julie hardly knew what to think. Was Della right about Larry's feelings? Julie cared for Larry very much. And of course she had wondered about whether they had a future together. But she had always kept her questions to herself, not wanting to assume anything about the relationship. She and Larry had never discussed getting married. And she knew him well enough to know that he would not discuss this subject with his mother, either. So, on what was Della basing her conjecture? Maternal instinct? Women's intuition? Suddenly Julie was nervous.

Della returned to the parlor with a note scrawled on scratch paper.

"Another reservation?" Julie asked.

"Yes. Looks like we'll be nearly full on the weekend."

"I'm sure I'll be over this soreness by then."

"Don't you even think about trying to help with meals!" Della shook a finger at Julie. "Your job is to rest till you're better. You can find plenty of things around here to amuse yourself."

"I'm so restless," Julie objected. "I want to get out and do something. Officer Rakes is not getting any closer to finding my paintings. Just sitting here waiting for something to happen is making me crazy!"

"I was really looking forward to having *Triumph* hanging at Leed House," Della said, shaking her head. "But I guess that might not happen."

Tears sprang to Julie's eyes. "Don't say that! It's a big painting. It can't just disappear. And there would be no point in stealing it just to destroy it."

"You've been thinking about this a lot, haven't you?"

"Every minute of the day. No matter what else is going on, I can't get *Triumph* out of my mind." She thumped her book on the coffee table.

"I know how much you loved your grandmother," Della said softly.

"Why did they have to take that painting?" Julie said, choking back a sob. "There was a whole roomful of paintings. Why that one?"

"It was the best thing you ever painted, Julie. Even an amateur like me could see that. It was more than a portrait. It was the story of a whole life told in colors on canvas."

"My grandmother's life. Her legacy to me." Awkwardly, Julie shifted her position and hugged a pillow against her chest. "I hate sitting here doing nothing. I even considered doing another portrait of Grammy. I tried to start a sketch. But it wasn't working. I don't want to do another portrait. I poured myself into *Triumph* and I want it back!"

Della moved to the sofa and sat down next to Julie. Gathering her young friend in her arms, she said, "We all want it back. But we can't change what happened."

Julie did not reply. Her mind was crying out with questions she dared not verbalize. *Why did God let all this happen in the first place? Couldn't He have stopped the theft? Couldn't He find the painting now? Why didn't He keep me safe in the storeroom that night?*

The doorbell rang and Julie pulled herself out of Della's arms.

fifteen

Della was back in a moment, with Charles Brooke striding in behind her, his sport coat slung over one shoulder. Julie thought he looked entirely too cheerful.

"Thought I'd come and check on the patient," he said as he lowered himself into the wooden rocking chair across from her. He flashed Julie a grin.

"It's a good thing you did," Della said. "This hasn't been one of her best days."

"Oh?" Charles raised one eyebrow at Julie.

Julie turned her head and looked out the window.

"I'm going to go start dinner while you two chat," Della said, excusing herself.

"What's going on?" Charles asked softly. His grin was gone. "Are you in pain?"

Julie shook her head. "Not most of the time. Only if I try to move too quickly."

"That brace looks pretty awkward." Charles was trying to be sympathetic.

"It is," Julie said sullenly. "And I'm getting really tired of this couch."

"You'll be up and around soon."

"Not soon enough." Involuntarily her lower lip went out in a pout.

"Della was right. You're not having a good day."

"Is that so hard to understand?" Julie snapped.

"Of course not."

Charles let the silence hang between them for a few moments. Julie twirled the fringe on a throw pillow around her finger, looking everywhere except at Charles.

"I see you have your sketch pad out," Charles said finally.

Julie tried to shrug, unsuccessfully. "Just trying to keep busy. I haven't been too productive."

"Mind if I look?"

"No. Go ahead."

Charles picked the pad up from the coffee table between them and began to turn the pages slowly. He paused over a sketch of a small town main street, similar to Seabridge, and a profile of Aunt Joanna. Then he turned to a caricature of Della and a fall view of the backyard.

"Looks to me like you've done a lot for just a couple of days."

"None of it is any good."

"Maybe it doesn't meet your standards, but it proves my point."

"What do you mean? What point?"

"About the light."

"What light?" Julie was curious, but a little impatient at the moment.

"The way you use light in all of your art. I mentioned it the other day. Considering your circumstances and your grumpy mood, you could have scribbled black masses. But these drawings are full of light."

Julie looked at him, puzzled. "No, they're not. That one of the backyard is full of the shadows of the end of the day. At least that's what I was trying to show."

"And you did. But look here, between the branches of the tree. The last of the light is seeping through and brightening everything in range."

"The main street is just gray," Julie persisted.

"But you included a street light. And it's on."

"It's a black-and-white drawing. How can you tell if the light is on."

"If it weren't on, there wouldn't be these shadows against

the storefronts."

Julie was silent. Charles had a point. She had not even realized herself how she had drawn the shadows in the path of the light.

Charles turned to the portrait of Aunt Joanna, her grandmother's old friend. "And look at this one. The shine from her eyes is incredible. It's as if the light could pierce right through me. I can only imagine what this would be like as a full-blown color portrait."

"I've said before that I just draw what I see."

"Then you have remarkable eyes. Your vision is a gift from God and I think you're trying to give it back to Him when you paint."

Julie did not know what to say to that. She had spent so many years struggling to understand her own gift and what it meant for her future. As hard as she worked on technique, she knew that her art was more than just hard work.

"Grammy used to tell me I had a gift from God, too," Julie said.

"I wish I could have known your grandmother. The woman in *Triumph* is a woman of faith."

"Do you really think so?" Julie looked directly at Charles for the first time in this conversation.

"That's the way you painted her. And you paint only what you see. You've said that yourself. I have to believe she knew God."

"She did." Julie hugged a pillow under her good arm. "There's so much about God that I don't understand," she said quietly.

"Who can understand God? If we could understand, we would not need Him." Charles leaned forward in his chair and rested his elbows on his knees. "Julie, don't let your lack of knowledge get in the way of expressing your faith."

"How can I believe things that I don't understand?"

"You paint things that you don't understand all the time."

"What do you mean?"

"Look at Aunt Joanna's eyes. Did you consciously sit down and analyze why her eyes are so bright? Were your strokes on the paper an act of understanding?"

Julie was listening carefully now.

"And think of *Triumph*. Did you analyze those images of your grandmother, or did you just paint what you knew to be true?"

Julie nodded slowly. She was beginning to understand.

"I think you're right. You draw what you see. But you see much more than you understand. That's part of what makes you an artist. Maybe faith is not so different from art."

"You're saying that I can believe more than I understand?"

"Absolutely."

"I sure don't understand why I had to lose *Triumph*. But what is it I'm supposed to believe from that experience?"

"That's a tough question. I know what that painting meant to you, and I'm not going to trivialize it with a pat answer about faith and how everything is in God's control. But keep thinking about it. You'll find your answer."

The pocket doors at the far end of the parlor slid open and Larry appeared.

"Hello, you two," he said. "Mom told me I'd find you both in here."

"Just thought I would stop by and check on things," Charles said, looking at Larry.

Julie felt oddly left out. She watched as the eyes of Charles and Larry met and some mysterious communication passed between them.

"Things are about the same," Larry said evenly.

"Perhaps today will bring some improvement," Charles replied.

Julie had reached her limit. "What is it with you two?" she demanded. "You're talking in some stupid code. Next, one of you is going to say something like 'Looks like rain today.'"

Charles glanced out the window. "Looks like rain this afternoon," he said.

Larry laughed.

Julie threw a pillow at Larry. "Don't make fun of me. What's going on? Wouldn't it be a lot easier to communicate with each other if you used plain English?"

Charles and Larry looked at each other, then back at Julie.

"Okay," Charles said. "I'll admit I had a second purpose in coming over here. I wanted to talk to Larry."

"About what?" Julie asked.

"About Dayton Edwards."

"What about him?" Larry asked, his interest heightened. He sat on the couch beside Julie.

"I talked some more with that guy at the car rental place. It turns out Dayton Edwards is a friend of a friend. He had some interesting things to say about Dayton's past."

"Like what?"

"He has a police record. For fraud and conspiracy."

Julie's jaw dropped open. "He's a criminal?"

Charles nodded. "He served a short sentence in the state penitentiary."

"I can't believe it," Julie said. Though she had found Dayton evasive on certain points, she had never suspected a criminal past.

"Well, I can believe it," Larry said. "Dayton Edwards is a charmer. I almost got taken in by him. But I knew there was more to his story than what we were hearing."

"And now we know," Charles said.

"Are you sure of these facts?" Larry questioned.

"Well, not completely," Charles admitted. "That's why I came by. I wondered if you wanted to come along while I check things out."

"Let me get my jacket."

"Wait, there's more."

Julie and Larry stared at Charles.

"What is it?" Larry asked.

"How much do you know about Fenway Lamp?"

Julie and Larry looked at each other.

"Not too much, actually," Julie answered. "He's been here four times now, I think. He usually stays two or three nights, but he keeps to himself and doesn't say much."

"That's right," Larry said. "In fact, Mom and I have wondered why he stays here. He seems like the sort that would be more comfortable in a hotel or a place where he can be more isolated."

"But why are we talking about Fenway Lamp?" Julie asked.

"Because he knew Dayton Edwards."

"Well, they were here together—"

"No, I mean they knew each other. Years ago."

"Are you sure? They hardly spoke to each other the whole four days they were here."

"I'm positive," Charles said. "Edwards and Lamp have known each other for at least seven years. Maybe longer."

"They gave absolutely no indication of that." Larry supported what Julie had already said.

"This is creepy," Julie said, shuddering slightly.

Charles nodded. "That's why I thought it was worth some investigating." He lifted an eyebrow at Larry. "Coming?"

"Of course," Larry answered quickly, standing up. Then he looked down at Julie, captive on the sofa. "You probably want to come, too."

She nodded.

"But you'd be better off here." His dark eyes were full of concern.

Julie met his gaze and nodded again. "I know."

"We have to get to the bottom of this." Larry stroked her shoulder gently.

"Yes. Go ahead. Just don't leave anything out when you get back."

Before she knew it, the men were gone and Julie was once again alone in the parlor with her book and a sketch pad.

Pulling an afghan across her lap and picking up her sketch pad, she settled back into a corner of the couch. Her restlessness was quelled for the time being. Charles's news represented progress, although meager. It was a lead that might take them nowhere. On the other hand, it might unleash a flow of information that would lead to *Triumph*. If all went well, Charles and Larry would bring back more solid information.

Feeling hopeful for the first time in two days, Julie reached for her pencil and opened the pad. Slowly, she flipped through the drawings Charles had studied. Gradually, she began to see the truth in what he had said. Light shone in all the drawings, a ray of hope illuminating the darkness of a small town and the shadows of old age.

She turned to the page Charles had not seen, the young woman reaching awkwardly for a doorknob. The forward grasp of her grandmother as a young woman jumped out at her, even though it was her own work. Suddenly the image was full blown in her mind and her pencil began to move.

The doorknob became a door swinging open. The young woman's face sparked hope and expectation as she looked through the open doorway. The picture did not show what was on the other side of the door. But what came from beyond, from the unknown, was a stream of light, both delicate and powerful. Its hues bathed the woman's face and swirled around her, nearly lifting her from the ground.

Julie worked for a long time, not noticing that grayness had invaded the parlor with the setting sun. When Della entered the room and snapped on a light, Julie could see the fruits of her labor and she was pleased.

sixteen

It was not until breakfast the next day that Julie saw Larry again. Wherever he and Charles had gone, they had stayed out late. Despite Julie's determination to wait up for Larry, she had given in to Della's insistence that she go to bed and get some sleep. She had a vague recollection of hearing a car in the driveway well after midnight but had not been able to rouse herself from the much-needed sleep that had overtaken her at last.

When Julie came downstairs on Wednesday morning, she found Larry sitting at the kitchen table, drinking coffee and reading a newspaper.

"Good morning," she said, trying not to sound overeager. She sat down across from him, in her usual spot. A tray of coffee mugs and napkins was between them on the table.

"Good morning," he responded brightly. "Did you sleep well?"

"Yes, I was more comfortable than I have been." She touched her side lightly. "Guess I'm getting used to this."

"That's good." He picked up his coffee mug and took a swallow. "Coffee?"

"Yes, please." She watched wordlessly as he stretched his long arm out to the counter behind him and grasped the coffeepot.

He filled a mug and pushed it toward her. "Here you go."

"Thanks. Where's Della?"

"Out for a walk. But she left cinnamon rolls in the oven. Want some?"

"Thanks, but I'm not hungry." This very polite morning exchange was making her impatient. Food was the last thing on her mind. "Well?" she said.

"Well, what?"

She scowled at him. "What happened yesterday? It was the middle of the afternoon when you and Charles left and you didn't come back until past midnight."

With an experienced motion, Larry refolded his newspaper and pushed it aside. Looking Julie in the eyes, he began his explanation. "Dayton Edwards used to work in an antique shop that Fenway Lamp owned. It was in southern New Hampshire. Charles and I talked with the police there last night."

"And?"

"And they were quite cooperative. They answered all our questions."

"So it's true. . .Dayton has a criminal past."

"He was quite a con man, apparently. He got involved in a ring of dealers who were passing off new furniture as restored antiques, at enormous profits."

"Did Mr. Lamp know?"

Larry shook his head. "As far as the police could tell, he was not involved. He claims that as soon as he discovered what Dayton was doing, he fired him. He's still selling antiques, although the shop in New Hampshire went bankrupt after the publicity about Dayton and the others. Dayton went to prison and Lamp relocated. According to the police, that was the end of the story."

"I suppose that would explain why Mr. Lamp acted like he didn't know Dayton while they were here."

"Maybe. But I'm not sure I could have remained as cool and collected as Lamp did if I met up with someone who had destroyed my business and ruined my reputation."

"You have a point," Julie said. She cocked her head to one side. "Does Officer Rakes know about Dayton's past?"

Larry shrugged. "I would think he did a police check on everyone at the time of the theft. But even if he does, he still has nothing to tie Dayton to everything that has been going on around here. The guy comes up as clean as a whistle."

"What happens now?" Julie wrapped her fingers around the warm mug. She was anxious to know how Dayton's past might bear on the events at the Flagg Gallery.

"I don't know," Larry said, shaking his head and refilling his coffee mug. "There's something fishy about Dayton Edwards, but I can't put my finger on it. Unless we find something that puts him under suspicion in this case, we may have come to the end of the road."

Julie's mind flashed to the morning she had seen Dayton and Vanessa talking in the parking lot outside Leed House. Was there more to that encounter than she thought?

"Larry, there may be something."

Larry locked his eyes on hers. "About Dayton?"

"I'm not sure. It was last week, a couple of days before the show. Do you remember the morning that Vanessa came by?"

"Of course. That was strange in itself."

"I was out in the gazebo that morning, sketching. I saw Dayton come out and talk to Vanni while she was still in her car."

"I remember. You mentioned it to Dan Rakes. But what was it about?"

"I couldn't hear. But it didn't look like an especially friendly conversation. Vanessa was not herself; I could see that much. I don't know what to make of it. I didn't even know they knew each other."

Larry's lower lip protruded as he thought. "Wasn't that the day that she hired him to help set things up?"

"I think so, yes."

"Maybe they had met earlier, somewhere in town."

"I suppose it's possible, but. . ."

"You're not persuaded."

"No." She shook her head adamantly. "Like you said, it was unusual that Vanni even came by that day."

"So you think she had another reason for coming by?"

"Maybe. At the time, it wasn't significant. I got involved with other things and just let it go. And I'm not sure it means anything now, either."

"Maybe we should snoop around to see about Vanessa's past, too."

Julie was shocked. "You can't be serious! Vanessa? A criminal?"

"You're too trusting, Julie."

"Vanessa Parker is my friend. She's been so helpful to me during the last year. I can't conceive of the idea that she was involved in any of this mess."

Larry reached across the table for Julie's hand. "Look, I didn't mean to upset you. You're probably right. I'm overly suspicious about everybody right now. Let's just forget it."

Her furor subsiding, Julie nodded. She distracted herself by drinking coffee.

"What do you say we take a day off today?" Larry's bright tone surprised Julie. But she quickly recognized his attempt to relax her nerves.

"A day off?" Julie asked.

"Yes, if you're up to it. We could go for a drive along the coast, have lunch somewhere, and be back before dinner."

"Are you sure your mother doesn't need you around here?"

"The bills are paid up and no guests are expected until tomorrow afternoon. Let's just go, get away from things for a while."

"That does sound appealing," she admitted.

"We'll take it slow and easy, no sudden movements. You can take your sketch pad. If it's not too blustery out, maybe we'll sit on the beach for a little while."

"You've got a deal. I'm ready to get out of the house."
Julie felt her shoulders relax. She needed a break from the
tension of the last few days. She turned to Larry and smiled.
"I think I'm ready for those cinnamon rolls now."

❧

The car moved smoothly along the coastal road, heading north.
When they set out after breakfast, Julie had hoped for a sun-
nier day but, even with a few shadowy clouds in the sky, the
weather was pleasant. With her head propped against the head-
rest, she turned her face to one side and watched, mesmer-
ized, as the ocean waves crashed against the rocks and sprayed
a mist into the air.

"The ocean is beautiful," Julie said simply. "I never get
tired of watching it."

"Why haven't you painted it more?" Larry asked.

"I have a hard time with it. It's so expressive, so powerful.
I can't seem to capture it well."

"You sold one seascape at the show, didn't you?"

"Yes. I could hardly believe David wanted to show that
one, but I guess he was right."

"Maybe you should try again."

"I'm sure I will eventually."

"I remember that day during your first summer here, when
I found you down at the beach in Seabridge, painting the
ocean."

Julie smiled. "I remember. I had made a fool of myself,
misinterpreting your friendship. You followed me down to
straighten me out."

Now Larry smiled. "You make it sound so harsh. I was
trying not to hurt you. Whatever became of that painting?"

"I destroyed it."

"Really? I didn't think you ever did that."

"I don't very often, but that painting was really bad."

"Or maybe it was your life that was bad at that point in

time. After all, you first came to Maine to get away from the stress at home in Illinois."

She turned her head to look at him as he drove. "There was so much family conflict over Grammy back then. My sister accused me of running away from things, but I just had to have a break."

"You deserved one. Your sister should give you credit for going back to help when your grandmother needed you."

"Don't forget about Dennis," Julie said, thinking of her college boyfriend. "He wanted something from me that I couldn't give. I had to get away and think for a while."

"Do you have any regrets about breaking up with him?" Larry glanced over at her and spoke softly.

Julie smiled and reached across the seat for his hand. "Only because I hurt him. I should have broken it off much sooner. I waited so long because I was having trouble letting go of things."

"Like your grandmother?"

"Right." She choked back a sob as she thought of the recent loss of *Triumph*. Perhaps she was still having trouble letting go of things.

"I suppose I complicated things for you that summer," Larry said.

"I complicated things for myself. My feelings about everything got out of hand. You wanted to be just friends."

He smiled. "Well, I guess I've changed my mind. I'm glad we moved past being just friends."

Julie held her breath and waited to see if he would say more. It was true that they were more than just friends. But what exactly were they? She wasn't quite sure. He did not say more.

"If my grandmother and your grandfather could see us now," she said, "I wonder what they would think."

"I'd like to think they would approve," Larry said confidently.

It's as if their romance is being played out again, two generations later, she thought. *But will it end any differently this time?*

"If they had been able to stay together," Larry said, "we wouldn't be us right now, and we wouldn't be having this conversation."

Julie laughed. "It's so strange to think about it that way. When I first read Grammy's diary, I felt so much hurt for her, like she had been wronged by her own parents. . .*my* great-grandparents. But I can't imagine not having the family I have."

"I guess it's impossible to imagine being someone else." Larry squinted out at the view. "What do you say? Shall we find a log and take in the grandeur of the sea?"

Julie quickly agreed to a visit to the beach. They parked the car, and Julie leaned on Larry as they slowly crossed the sand. They had no trouble finding a dry hunk of driftwood on which to sit. Julie held her sketch pad on her lap. She had not decided yet if she would draw, but she wanted to be prepared, as always.

They sat contentedly side by side on the short piece of driftwood, watching the waves billow and burst and creep back out to the depths once again. When the wind gusted, Larry put his arm around Julie's shoulder and pulled her closer.

"Are you warm enough out here?"

She nodded, her senses saturated with satisfaction. "This is great. Soon it will really be too cold to come out here. I'm glad we did this."

They sat in silence for a while again.

"Charles seems to like you a lot," Larry said, quite unexpectedly.

Julie turned and looked at him, her eyebrows raised.

"He's going the extra mile to try to figure out who took your paintings," Larry continued. "And I've been spending more time with him than usual. He mentions you a lot."

Julie was not sure what to say. It crossed her mind that perhaps Larry was jealous. He had no way of knowing that her conversations with Charles revolved around her resistance to doing a painting for the church narthex.

"I suppose we have gotten to know each other a little better lately," she said cautiously. "But most of what we talk about is church stuff."

Larry nodded but did not say anything. He just stared out at the sea.

Julie had the distinct feeling that he had more to say. She also just stared out at the thundering water.

"Julie, I hope you know how much you mean to me," Larry said. "When I found you in that storeroom unconscious. . .I should never have let you go into the shop alone that night."

"It's not your fault I got hurt."

"I'm going to do everything I can to make sure it doesn't happen again. And I hope you'll stay at Leed House for a long, long time."

"I don't have any plans to leave."

"Good."

The feeling persisted that there was more on Larry's mind than he was revealing.

Larry stood up. "Come on. Mom will have a fit if she finds out I dragged you down to sit on driftwood. And it's getting cold."

Julie laughed. "Della's presence has a long reach."

"Let's find that place with the great homemade soup," Larry said, taking her hand and pulling her to her feet.

Whatever he had on his mind would remain unsaid. As they walked back to the car, Julie squeezed his hand tightly.

seventeen

The family-run restaurant renowned for its homemade soups and breads proved a welcome refuge from the gusty outdoors. But in its open seating and brightly colored dining room, the mood between Larry and Julie lightened. Over lunch they chatted about scenery and favorite vacation memories and places they would like to visit someday. Slurping soup and sampling breads, they relaxed and let go of the tensions of the past week. For the first time since the theft, Julie was free from the weight of her loss. Somehow she had managed to let go for a few hours.

In the truck on the way home, they were quiet. Their conversation that day had swung in extreme directions and now the pendulum had come to a silent center. Julie wondered what Larry was thinking about, but she did not ask.

As they approached Seabridge, Larry broke the silence and turned to Julie. "Do you want to stop in town for anything?"

She hesitated only briefly before answering. "Actually, I would like to stop at the shop for a few minutes."

"Oh? Are you sure you're up to that?"

"Yes, I am. Vanni hasn't even called since closing night." Now that they were back in town, Julie's mind was turning back to the realities at hand. "David, of course, always has business on his mind, but I had hoped I would hear from Vanni. Something is not right."

"Okay, then, we'll stop."

A few minutes later, Larry parked the truck in front of the shop and they went in. Vanessa was busy selling a set of small prints to a customer. Julie wriggled her fingers in greeting, but Vanni seemed not to notice. David was nowhere in sight. While she waited for Vanessa, Julie wandered toward the back of the store, past the little desk that she sometimes used. Still no David. But, propped against the wall, were the unsold paintings, with a note taped to one frame.

> *Julie,*
> *Do you want to keep any of these? I'll sell*
> *the others.*
>
> *D.*

The question was the reason she had been in the shop looking for a box at the same time that an intruder was in the storeroom.

Larry followed her back. "What are you doing back here?" he asked.

Involuntarily, she jumped at the sound of his voice. "I thought David might be here, but I don't see him."

She had her hand on the knob of the storeroom door.

"Julie—"

Larry tried to stop her, but she could not resist the urge to look in the storeroom. She pushed open the door and the light from the hall seeped into the storeroom. Without turning on more light, she glanced around. The shelves had been righted and everything put away. In fact, the whole room was more organized than it had been before her injury. There was no evidence of the incident.

"Everything is back to business in here," she muttered.

"Don't put yourself through this, Julie," Larry cautioned.

"I'm all right," she assured him, closing the door. "There's nothing to see in there anyway."

The cash register dinged and she glanced up to see that

Vanessa was free now. The front door swung closed behind the departing customer. Julie started back up to the front of the store.

"Hi, Vanessa!"

"Hi, there," Vanni replied. "I thought you were still home in bed."

"I got restless. Larry rescued me from my misery today. We went for a drive and had lunch."

"Sounds nice."

"It was." Julie was mystified at the curt response. Vanessa usually chattered at a fairly steady speed. Today, Vanessa hardly looked up from her work at the register.

Julie forged on. "I was wondering about the show. . .how it all came out."

"Do you mean sales?"

"Yes. How well did we do?"

. "You did beautifully. David and I did all right, too."

"I'm so relieved," Julie said with a sigh. "The two of you went out on a limb for me. I was afraid it wouldn't be worth your while."

Vanessa fished on the shelf under the counter for something. "I've got the total here somewhere. Yes, here." She laid a piece of yellow paper on the counter for Julie to read .

"That much?" Julie questioned. She could not believe the figure she saw.

Larry leaned over her shoulder to see for himself. "That's pretty impressive."

"That's the total sales," Vanessa explained. "You get the percentage stated in our contract." She turned back to the cash register and broke open a roll of quarters.

"That's still a lot," Julie said, still staring at the piece of paper.

"We got a lot of press coverage, too. Two trade magazines

have called. One wants to run a short piece on the show and the other wants to do a feature on you." She fished under the counter again and came up with a pink telephone message slip. "Here. This is a number to call if you're interested in the interview."

"Thanks." Julie was flattered by the idea of a feature article, but at the moment she was more concerned about the fact that Vanessa was clearly distracted. Although the news she delivered was good, her tone was less than enthusiastic.

"David will have to talk to you about the commissions," Vanessa said matter-of-factly.

"Commissions?"

"Yes, two clients are interested in commissioning something."

Vanessa straightened a stack of papers on the counter and then moved to her own antique oak desk against the side wall behind the register. Her back was to Julie now, and she quickly absorbed herself in her paperwork.

Julie looked at Larry, who shrugged in response. Vanni's behavior did not make sense. Her reputation as a salesperson was built on her friendliness and personal charm. Julie's relationship with Vanessa had always been warm and comfortable. Her disappointment that Vanessa had not called during the last two days magnified now.

Larry nudged her elbow and nodded his head toward Vanessa. He was right, Julie decided. She could not just walk away from this without finding out what was going on. She approached Vanni's desk and tried to get her friend's attention.

"Vanessa? Is everything all right?"

"Of course, Julie." Vanessa looked up and finally smiled at Julie. But the expression did not feel real. "I'm just swamped with paperwork right now. We're still catching up after the show."

"So you're okay?" Julie asked again.

"Of course I'm okay. You're the one who got hurt. You should be home taking it easy. Let Della pamper you."

"She has been."

Vanessa stood up and walked down the side aisle where the art supplies were hanging on racks on the wall. She had a pad of paper and started taking inventory of the depleted stock.

"I could help you with that," Julie offered. "I've done the inventory before."

"Thanks, but that's not necessary."

The front door opened and a customer entered.

"Can I help you?" Vanessa called out, walking toward the young man.

"I need some charcoal pencils and a couple of sketch pads."

"Right over here." Vanessa led the customer to the appropriate spot and engaged in a serious conversation about charcoal pencils.

"This is weird," Julie whispered to Larry. "Vanessa hates selling art supplies. She thinks it distracts from the real business of the gallery."

"She's obviously avoiding you," Larry said flatly.

"But why? What did I do?"

"Maybe it's not something that you did."

"What do you mean?"

"Maybe it's something Vanessa did. . .or didn't do." His voice was low and controlled.

Julie's eyebrows furrowed. "You're not getting suspicious of Vanni again, are you?" she whispered.

"You said yourself that she's acting weird."

Vanessa and the customer approached the counter. Larry and Julie stood mutely aside while Vanessa rang up the sale. The young man began fingering the post cards on the rack on the counter and asked a series of trivial questions. Julie thought he would never leave the store. Finally he was gone. Vanessa gave a faint smile at Julie and returned to the aisle to continue her inventory. Julie followed her, determined.

"I can see you're busy now," Julie said, "but maybe we could get together soon. . .have dinner or something."

Vanessa nodded awkwardly. "Maybe in a couple of weeks. I'll be working a lot of extra hours for a while."

Julie nodded wordlessly. She still wanted an explanation. "Vanessa—"

"I'll tell David you were here," Vanessa said, cutting Julie off. "I'm sure he'll be sorry he missed you."

"Well, tell him I'll stop by again soon. Or he can call me any time."

"Great. I'll tell him. Glad you're feeling better." Vanessa reached out to count a stack of small red paint jars.

Julie glanced over at Larry, who gestured that they should just leave. Silently, she followed him out.

&

She sat at the oak kitchen table with Della and Larry, picking at her dinner and hardly hearing the conversation around her. Vanessa's behavior was beyond understanding. Julie could think of nothing in recent days that should have alerted her that she had offended her friend. Overnight, Vanessa's attitude toward their relationship had soured. Clearly, she did not even want Julie to linger around the shop, as she so often had in the last year and a half. Did Vanessa see Julie as the reason for all the recent trouble? How could Julie comfortably continue to work with David if Vanessa resented her presence?

She pushed her mashed potatoes to one side of the plate as she pondered these questions.

"Julie, are you all right?" Della asked.

"Hmm?" She looked up at Della.

"I asked if you're feeling all right."

"I feel fine. A little tired maybe."

"You haven't eaten a bite. Did you have a big lunch?"

"Just soup."

"Then you need to eat."

Julie set her fork down. "I can't. Not until I know what's going on with Vanessa."

"Obviously she did not want to talk about it," Larry said.

"I don't care. I'm entitled to an explanation of why I'm suddenly so undesireable as a friend."

"You can't force her to talk to you."

"I can try," she said with determination.

"What are you going to do?"

"I'm going over to her apartment." She tossed her napkin on the table. "Right now."

"You shouldn't be driving," cautioned Della.

"I'll walk, then."

"It's cold and dark out there," Larry said sensibly. "You're in no condition to walk two miles to her apartment. I'll drive you."

"Okay, but you'll have to wait for me in the car. I don't want to give Vanessa any reason to avoid talking to me."

"I understand."

"Let's go."

eighteen

"Are you sure you don't want me to go up with you?" Larry asked, as he slowed the truck to the curb in front of Vanessa's apartment building. He snapped off the headlights.

"I'm sure," Julie nodded. "I think I can get her to talk to me if we are alone."

"It's too cold to sit in the truck," Larry said as he took the key out of the ignition. "I'll be in the coffee shop across the street."

Julie laughed nervously. "This could take a while. They might think you're loitering. You'll have to order a lot of pie and coffee."

Larry patted his stomach. "No problem."

"Okay," she said, putting her hand on the door handle. "Here I go."

She waved to Larry as he crossed the street and slipped into the brightly lit diner.

Taking a deep breath to calm her nerves, Julie pulled open the heavy door to the old brick building and entered the shadowy foyer. She had been there many times; her finger knew right where to find the buzzer for Vanessa's rear apartment.

After a few seconds, the speaker clicked. "Yes?" came Vanessa's voice.

"Vanni, it's me, Julie."

After an unnatural pause, Vanessa asked, "What do you need?"

"I'd like to come up and talk."

"Well. . .this is not really a good time. I was going to go to bed early."

"Please, Vanni, let me come up."

The speaker clicked off and the door to the stairwell buzzed open. Julie grabbed it before Vanessa could change her mind.

Vanessa met her in the hallway upstairs. She had shed the sleek navy suit of earlier in the day in favor of rumpled, baggy sweats. Julie had never seen her friend looking so disheveled. Normally even Vanessa's casual wear was on the leading edge of fashion. She looked completely out of character in gray, formless clothing.

"Are you feeling all right?" Julie asked.

"I'm still tired out from that bug last week, I guess," Vanessa said.

"I'm sorry to disturb you, but I think it's important that we talk."

Vanessa nodded. Her face was nearly colorless, alarming Julie. "Come on in," Vanni said.

Julie stepped into the apartment. Despite Vanessa's appearance, she was still expecting the impeccable orderliness she usually found in Vanessa's cozy home. Instead, carefully placed knickknacks were buried under magazines haphazardly tossed around the living room. A pile of dirty laundry ornamented the hall. Soiled dishes were scattered around the corners of the room, with a noticeable pile in the kitchen sink.

Vanessa noticed Julie's eye movements. "Sorry about the mess," she mumbled. "I just haven't been myself lately."

"I'm sorry. I didn't know," Julie said. "If I had known you were still feeling so bad—"

"You couldn't have done anything to help." Vanessa cut her off. "You've had enough of your own problems lately."

"Still. . .I. . .would like to have known." Julie did not know what else to say.

"I'll fix some tea," Vanessa said, more out of habit than enthusiasm. "Go ahead and sit down."

Vanessa busied herself in the kitchenette. Julie moved Vanessa's raincoat out of an easy chair and sat down awkwardly.

"Do you want some help?" Julie asked.

"No." Vanessa's voice was flat. Her back was to Julie; she did not even look over her shoulder as she spoke.

Julie did not attempt further conversation. Self-consciously, she glanced over at the stove, waiting for the water to boil. Finally, Vanessa finished making tea and handed her a steaming mug.

"I put a lot of honey in it, the way you like," Vanessa said.

"Thanks." Julie took a cautious sip of the hot liquid as Vanessa dropped into the couch across from her. She had not poured herself any tea.

"Vanessa," Julie began, "I was hoping we could talk tonight, just the two of us."

"Well, there's no one else here."

"We haven't really had a talk to catch up on things lately," Julie said, feeling as feeble as she sounded.

"I don't really have much else to report about the show. I told you all I know when you came by the store today."

"I appreciated the information," Julie said deliberately, "but that's not what I meant."

"What, then?"

"I wanted us to just talk. The show sort of took over everything for a while, but it's over now."

"I'm still going to be really busy."

Julie set her mug down, on a cluttered end table, with a thud. "Vanni, what's going on?" she demanded.

"Nothing's going on. If I sound crabby, it's because I'm tired."

"It was obvious today that you didn't want me around. And don't tell me it was my imagination. Larry could see it, too."

"I don't know what you're talking about." Vanessa said.

She started straightening the quilt that was wadded up on one end of the couch. "I just had a lot to do today, that's all."

Julie got up and grabbed one end of the quilt to stop Vanessa's activity.

"Look at this place," Julie said. "It's a disaster zone. That's not like you."

"I've been too busy to clean." Vanessa tugged at the quilt again.

"Vanessa, look at me. You haven't really looked me in the eye since I came in the door."

Vanessa kept her eyes on the quilt and did not speak for a long time. "I can't," she finally whispered hoarsely.

"Why not?" Julie's tone softened. "We've been good friends for more than a year. We've talked about a lot of intimate things. Why can't you look at me?"

"Because I don't want you to hate me." Vanessa's voice was barely audible. She sank back into the couch and hugged the quilt to her chest.

Julie sat next to her and reached out for Vanessa's hand. "Why would I hate you? You're one of the best friends I've ever had."

Vanessa sniffled and turned her head away. "Then I think you need to look for new friends. You could do a lot better."

"I'm not leaving until I get to the bottom of this," Julie said stubbornly. "You might as well make it easy on us both and tell me what's going on right now."

There was a long pause. Neither of them moved.

"I left the security alarm off that night," Vanessa said quietly. "The night your paintings were taken."

"Oh." Julie let the words sink in. "But you told Officer Rakes that you locked everything up as usual."

"I lied."

"You lied? Why would you do that?" Julie grappled for an explanation. "It was a mistake, that's all. You're human like the rest of us."

"It was a mistake all right, but it was not an accident."

"I don't understand, Vanni. What are you saying?"

"I'm saying I knew the theft was going to happen, and I let it happen. I made it easy."

Julie felt a strange pressure building in her chest, and her head filled with more questions than she could process. "Maybe you'd better start at the beginning," she finally managed to say.

"The beginning was a long time ago," Vanessa said quietly, having regained her composure. "I was young. I did some stupid things. . .petty theft, conning people out of things."

The picture was starting to come together for Julie. "You didn't happen to know Dayton Edwards back then, did you?"

Vanessa nodded. "We pulled a few jobs together. You know about his past, I guess."

"I know he went to jail for fraud and that he had been working for Fenway Lamp at the time."

"Fortunately I was not involved in the job that sent him to jail, so I came out of it clean. After that, when Fenway Lamp wanted me to keep working for him, I refused. I knew I had to straighten out my life."

"Wait a minute," Julie said. "You mean Fenway Lamp was involved in this shady business?"

"He was running it," Vanessa answered. "I'll never understand how he managed to avoid being arrested. He is so slick."

"I just found out about Dayton today," Julie said. "But the police in New Hampshire said they didn't suspect Mr. Lamp of anything."

"That's the incredible part."

"But if you walked away from all that, what does that have to do with my paintings."

Vanessa stood up and started pacing. "I'm so disgusted with myself. I can't even bring myself to say the words."

Julie pressed her lips together and forced herself to be patient.

"Fenway Lamp showed up in town a few months ago," Vanni began.

"I know. He has stayed at Leed House several times."

"That was innocent enough, I guess," Vanessa said, shrugging. "There's a legitimate side to his business, and that's what he was here for."

"And?"

"And he wandered into the store one day. I hadn't seen him in all these years and suddenly there he was. The next time he came to town he came to see me again. By then he had heard about your show. He actually admires your work quite a bit. And he's got a good eye for art."

"I'm not sure how to take that."

"The point is that he thinks you're going to hit it big, and he thought that if he had a few of your early works that they'd be worth a lot of money."

"That's ridiculous. I'm virtually an unknown."

"That's why he wanted a no-risk form of investment."

"I see. Stealing doesn't cost him anything."

"Right. But he needed help."

"And you gave it to him."

Tears oozed out of both of Vanessa's puffy eyes as she nodded. Julie fought for self-control; she did not want to collapse into an emotional heap at this moment, no matter what the truth turned out to be.

"Why?" Julie asked. "Why would you help him? You're successful in what you do."

"I've spent the last seven years building up a reputation of my own," Vanessa said, choking. "I love what I do. But David Flagg is pure professionalism. His gallery is above reproach. Do you think for one moment that he would let me keep working for him if he knew about my past?"

"Lamp was blackmailing you?"

Vanessa nodded. "I said no two times. But then he had lunch with David and made quite an impression on him. I got scared. And Fenway is not used to people saying no to him. I nearly had to run for my life seven years ago. I was afraid of what he would do to me."

"You mean, you thought he would hurt you. . .physically?"

"I wouldn't put it past him." Vanessa swallowed a sob. "Julie, I never meant for you to get hurt. And I never thought he would take *Triumph!* He was just supposed to take a few landscapes. He said he had casually discussed insurance with David one day and knew that everything was covered. Nobody was going to get hurt. The Flagg Gallery would still get its money, and he would have a little hedge against a future Julie Covington fad."

Julie did not know what to say. She still had dozens of questions. "On closing night, in the storeroom. . .was that him?"

"I think so. I wouldn't be able to prove it, but he might have come back."

Julie was overwhelmed. "I never expected you to say anything like this tonight."

"Now that I've said it out loud, it sounds absurd," Vanessa said, still pacing. "I can't believe I actually went along with this scheme." She punched the wadded up quilt angrily. "If only he hadn't taken *Triumph*."

"Was Dayton Edwards in on this?" Julie asked. "Is that why he was so anxious to work around the gallery when we were setting up?"

Vanessa shook her head. "Dayton knew about it. Fenway wanted him to do the job, but he refused."

"He refused?" Julie repeated incredulously. All the information Charles and Larry had uncovered painted a picture of Dayton that would make his involvement likely.

"Dayton has gone straight. He's been completely

legitimate since he got out on parole."

"Then why was he here now?" Julie probed.

"To try to stop it. He insisted that I meet him at Leed House that morning. I didn't want to talk to him, but I was afraid that he would tip off David if I didn't. So I came. He was trying to talk me out of it, and he wanted Lamp to know he was trying, so he wanted to be visible."

Julie sank back in the couch, hardly able to believe what she was hearing.

"Dayton even wanted to set the alarm," Vanessa continued, "but he didn't know the codes. It's my fault. Everything that happened is my fault."

Julie was coming to her senses. She stood up and stepped in front of Vanessa's pacing. "You have to tell the police. Dan Rakes can track down Fenway Lamp—"

"No!" Vanessa said loudly. "I can't do that."

Julie grasped Vanni by the shoulders and looked into her eyes. "Then I will."

Vanessa's shoulders sagged. "I suppose there's no way out now. David will fire me and I'll end up in jail as an accessory to a crime."

"Vanessa, I'm no legal expert. I don't know what's going to happen to you. But you have to do the right thing this time."

Vanessa searched Julie's eyes for understanding. "You haven't screamed at me or anything. I betrayed you and caused you to lose something you really care about. And you're so calm."

"Vanessa, I do care about *Triumph*. And maybe now we can get it back. But more than that, I care about you."

Vanessa rummaged in her pocket for a ragged tissue and blew her nose. "This is tearing me up, Julie. I can't keep up the facade any longer. Call Dan Rakes."

nineteen

"Is it true?" Charles Brooke burst through the parlor doors with his eyes wide. "Did you find the paintings?" He looked rumpled and haggard, yet fully alert.

"Slow down, Charles," Larry said. "The paintings are still missing, but at last we have a real lead."

"My people are checking into it right now," Officer Dan Rakes said solemnly.

"Do you want some coffee?" Della asked, ever the gracious hostess.

"Yes, black, please," Charles said gratefully. He turned to Larry. "What's the story? I want all the facts."

"I would advise against that," Officer Rakes said. "Let's keep a lid on this until we recover the items."

Della handed Charles his coffee. "Does anyone need a refill?"

The cacophony of voices took Julie to her tolerance level. "Wait a minute," she said. "It's after midnight. Charles, how did you find out about this? It just happened a few hours ago."

"I was at the church working late. I stopped by the diner on my way home and Alyce told me."

"Alyce?"

"You know. The waitress with the red hair."

"Oh, yes," Larry said, turning to Julie. "She's the one who answered the phone when you called me there from Vanessa's. Guess she was eavesdropping."

"But she didn't get it quite right," Charles said, disappointed.

"By morning, the whole town will think the paintings are back," Julie said. "But they're not. So much for keeping a lid on things."

"My people are checking into it," Dan Rakes repeated.

"Just exactly what are they checking?" Charles asked.

Dan eyed him suspiciously. "Miss Parker has provided solid information for our investigation. We'll take care of things from here." He turned to Julie. "Miss Covington, if there is nothing else you can remember about your conversation with Vanessa Parker, I'll be on my way. I'll be in touch as soon as we know something."

"Are you going to arrest Vanessa?"

"The district attorney's office will decide that. I have already advised her to seek legal counsel." He nodded in Della's direction. "Thanks for the coffee. I'll see myself out."

When they heard the front door shut behind him, Charles turned to the others. "I want to know what happened tonight."

For the third time in two hours, Julie recounted the gist of her conversation with Vanessa, highlighting the role of Fenway Lamp.

"So Dayton Edwards had nothing to do with it?" Charles asked.

Julie shook her head. "Just that he was trying to warn Vanessa to stay out of it."

"I feel terrible," Larry said. "I was so suspicious of him. It never crossed my mind that Fenway Lamp could possibly be involved in something like this."

"If we ever track him down, we'll apologize," Charles said. "In the meantime, I found Fenway Lamp. He lives in Vermont, near where David Flagg's mother lives."

"So he's the one who sent that fax about his mother being ill," Julie said.

"Looks that way. At least, he had it sent. . .he was already here. He needed David out of the way for the night. That was the only way he could get to Vanessa."

"Wait a minute," Della said. "If Fenway Lamp is stealing things, he wouldn't be stupid enough to store them in an obvious place, like where he lives."

"It's not quite that simple," Charles conceded, "but almost. A few months back, at a church potluck, I heard Harold say something about having rented storage space to a man from out of town."

"So?" asked Julie.

Before Charles could answer, Larry jumped in. "You think it was Fenway Lamp, don't you?"

Charles nodded. "At the time, I didn't think anything of it. Harold rents space to a lot of people. But it came up again the other day. He made some comment about the things the man was putting in the storage room. Harold thought it was a bunch of old junk."

"Antiques," Julie said.

"Or potential fake antiques," Larry added.

"Right," Charles said.

"This is ridiculous," Della insisted. "Fenway Lamp would not be foolish enough to hide stolen goods right in the same little town where he stole them."

"You're right, of course," Charles agreed. "But if he rented storage space in one small town—"

"He probably has space in other towns, too." The puzzle was coming together for Julie at last.

Charles was nodding. "Exactly."

"It's a completely legitimate idea," Larry said. "Rather than transporting goods he may never need for his business, he rents inexpensive storage space. I'll bet he does business all over New England this way."

"Oh, great," Julie moaned. "Then how are we ever going

to figure out where else he might have space?"

"It might take some time," Charles said, "but the antique network is pretty close knit. If any part of his activity is legitimate, other dealers will know him and where he does business."

"We'll just have to start asking around," Larry said.

"Shouldn't we talk to Officer Rakes about this?" Julie asked quite sincerely. "Are you sure we should head off in our own direction?"

"Rakes will just say that his men are checking everything out," Charles said. "He won't say what they are investigating."

"I'm sure he doesn't want to compromise any leads they have."

"My guess is that he has dispatched someone down to Vermont to look for Lamp, rather than looking first for the paintings."

"You may be right, but still. . . What if it gets dangerous?" Julie persisted in her doubts. "What will you do if you find the paintings. . .or Lamp?"

Charles and Larry looked at each other and shrugged.

"We'll just take one step at a time," Charles said. "We'll worry about that when it happens."

Julie looked to Larry for confirmation.

"We'll be sensible, Julie," he said, answering her unspoken question. "I think Charles is right; we should get moving on this right away."

"That's all fine and good," Della pronounced as she stood up and started stacking coffee cups. "But it's one o'clock in the morning. The antique dealers I know would not appreciate being bothered at this hour."

"Mom is right," Larry agreed. "We can't do much tonight. We should try to get some sleep." He turned to Charles. "Why don't you just stay in one of the empty rooms tonight and we'll get started first thing in the morning."

"That's a wonderful idea," Della said. "I'll show you to your room."

Charles glanced from Larry to Della and said, "I guess it's been decided. I'll stay."

"Follow me." Della led the way up the stairs to the second floor, leaving Larry and Julie alone in the parlor.

"I want to go with you, you know," Julie said firmly.

"I know, I know. You have every right to come along. But I would hate myself if you got hurt. . .again."

"A few minutes ago you assured me you would be sensible. Nobody should get hurt. If that's the case, I'm in no danger. I can handle riding in the back seat of a car."

Larry pulled Julie to her feet and put his arms around her. "It's going to be all right, Julie. We'll find *Triumph*."

"I hope you're right," she mumbled into his shoulder.

"I'll walk you up to your room," he said.

"Okay, but wake me as soon as you get up."

❧

Once upstairs, Julie went through the motions of getting ready for bed, but she was sure she would not sleep.

She slept five hours. When she woke it was almost six-thirty. Julie splashed some cold water on her face and scrambled into fresh jeans and a sweater and nearly bounded down the two flights of stairs to the kitchen.

Coffee was brewing and the newspaper was spread out on the table.

"Larry?" she called out. "Charles?"

Della appeared from the pantry. "Good morning, Julie. Did you get some sleep?"

Julie nodded. "More than I thought I would. Isn't Larry up yet? Shouldn't we wake him?"

Della quietly poured a mug of coffee and handed it to Julie. "They're gone. About forty minutes ago."

"Gone? But I specifically told Larry to wake me up when he got up. He knew I wanted to go along."

"It's my fault," Della said. "He started to go knock on your door and I put my foot down. It's bad enough that you went gallivanting all over the county yesterday. You're not taking care of yourself. I insisted that he leave you here."

"Della! How could you?" Julie had never been angry with Della before. It was a strange feeling, but she could not suppress it. "How dare you treat me like a child! That was my choice to make."

"I know. I'm sorry. I don't think it would have been sensible for you to go running around the countryside, but I should have persuaded you, not Larry."

Julie sighed. Though the disappointment would linger, the edge of her fury was softening. Certainly nothing could be done about the situation now.

"Can I pry forgiveness from you with a hot breakfast?" Della pleaded. "I've got fresh bran muffins in the oven, just about ready to come out."

Julie stuck her lower lip out in a pout. "Only if you put honey on them."

"I wouldn't think of serving them any other way." Della picked up a potholder and opened the oven.

❧

The morning was a long one. Della busied herself cleaning guest rooms and making a shopping list for the weekend menus. Julie wandered from one room to another, restless and anxious.

"Have those two forgotten how to use a phone?" she asked Della just before lunch.

As if on cue, the phone rang. Julie sprang to answer it.

"Hello? Larry?"

After a pause, a voice answered. "No, it's me."

"Vanessa?"

"Yes. I just wanted to see how you are today."

"I'm okay. Thanks to you, I may get *Triumph* back. How are you doing?"

"I slept better than I have in two weeks. I guess a clean conscience makes a difference."

"I'm so glad you finally told me what had happened," Julie said softly. "And not just because of the paintings, but because we're friends."

"Are we still? I mean, after what I did—"

"The important thing is that you finally told the truth. If you didn't care about me, you could have kept it all to yourself."

"How can you possibly forgive me, Julie? I can hardly forgive myself."

"I've done some stupid things in my life, too. Everyone deserves another chance."

"Is there any word on *Triumph*?" Vanessa asked.

"The police are looking for Mr. Lamp, and Larry and Charles took off this morning with some ideas about where he may have left the paintings."

"I wish I could help you there. But I didn't want to know anything more about his business than I had to."

"Of course not."

"I'll get off the phone in case someone is trying to call you."

"We'll talk later," Julie said, wishing she had the right words to comfort the hurting friend who was also her betrayer.

❧

In the early afternoon, Julie picked at her lunch and finally decided to go up to her tower room and rest. Outside, the day was brisk and windy. Undaunted, Julie raised the window, pushed open the shutters, and let the fall air in. The sunlight came also, seeping in and changing the tint of the room. A white cast settled over the furniture as leaves outside rustled in the breeze. She settled into her big chair under the window. She laid her head back on the chair, where her face could catch a bit of winter warmth. Soon she felt calmer than she had all day and began to imagine in her mind a painting that would capture the feeling of the security that she felt just then.

But what had brought on the change? Why was she so calm? Was it really the light from outside the window? Or was it the faith that Charles insisted she had inside her even when she herself could not find it? Her mind wandered to the sketch of her grandmother as a young woman opening the door to the unknown. In a full-scale painting, she would be able to flood the room with hues of vibrating light. Light would come from the unknown and infuse its perspective through everything about the young woman. Was this faith?

A blaring horn jerked her to her feet. Hanging out the tower window, she saw Larry's car squeal joyfully into the driveway. She waved her arm out the window, then turned and hurried down the stairs.

twenty

By the time Julie reached Larry's car, Della was already outside, conducting an interrogation. "Where have you two been?" Della asked emphatically. "Why didn't you call? Did you find the paintings? Did you find Mr. Lamp? I'll tell you one thing: I'll make sure he never stays at Leed House again or anywhere else in Seabridge."

Larry laid a hand on his mother's shoulder. "Mom, slow down for just a minute and we'll tell you everything we know."

"You'd better!" Julie said. "If you only knew how angry I am at you for leaving me behind!"

Larry looked at her sheepishly. "Sorry about that. But right now there are more important things to discuss."

"Did you get *Triumph* back?" She looked from Larry to Charles anxiously.

"Yes and no," Charles answered.

"Just give me the facts," Julie demanded.

"All of them?"

"The ones that matter."

"The most important fact is that, yes, we did find *Triumph*." Julie jumped and a squeal escaped. "Where is it?" She started to push past the group to look in Larry's car.

"We don't exactly have it," Larry said, catching her elbow.

"Where exactly is it?"

"We went through several towns around here where antique dealers do a lot of business. We finally tracked down some rented space that sounded like it could be Lamp's. So we went to look for ourselves."

Julie's eyes widened. "Did you break in?"

Larry and Charles looked at each other nervously. "We thought about it," Charles admitted. "Fortunately, we didn't have to face that decision. The police were already there."

"The police?"

"Yep. Turns out Dan Rakes knew what he was doing after all," Charles conceded sheepishly. "I should have had more confidence in his investigation."

"More faith?" Julie chided playfully.

Charles grinned.

Larry continued the explanation. "By the time we got there, Dan had arrested Lamp in Vermont and already had a warrant to search the premises."

"And *Triumph* was there?"

"Yes, and the landscapes, too.

"Where are they now?"

"Dan impounded them as evidence, so I'm afraid it will be a while before you actually get them back."

Julie's whole body sagged with relief. "At least I know they're safe now."

They all turned as another car pulled into the long driveway.

"Here's Dan now," Larry said. The classic black-and-white police car slowed to a stop and Officer Rakes emerged with his usual casual saunter.

"Good morning, Mrs. Paxton, Miss Covington," he said. "I imagine you've heard the news by now."

"We certainly have," Della answered. "We're delighted that you found the paintings, of course. But isn't there some way for Julie to get them back? Must you keep them?"

"I'm afraid so," he answered. "As soon as the trial is over, you can have them back."

"That could take months!" Julie protested.

"Maybe longer," Dan added. "But we have a good case against this Lamp fellow. Your friend Miss Parker has agreed to testify against him in exchange for lesser charges against her. You will get your paintings back."

"I guess there's no choice here; it'll be a long time before we see *Triumph* again," Julie said with finality, her head drooping.

"Oh, you can *see* the paintings," Dan said. "In fact, I need you to identify them for the record."

Julie snapped her head up. "When? Where are they?"

Dan nodded toward his car. "I've got them here, in the trunk." He stepped around to the back of the car and unlocked the trunk. Julie eagerly looked over his shoulder. There, wrapped carefully in clear plastic, was *Triumph*. Under the large painting, the two small landscapes were squarely set in the bottom of the trunk.

Dan lifted the large frame and pulled back the plastic. "Is this the painting that was stolen from the Flagg Gallery?"

Julie nodded, tears filling her eyes. "Yes. It is. All three of them are mine."

Larry came up behind her and put an arm across her shoulders. Together they looked at *Triumph*. Her grandmother, Julienne Leed Covington, stared back at them from the central image on the canvas.

Della and Charles joined them. "Do you know how much you look like your grandmother?" Charles asked.

Julie nodded. "People always said that about us."

"It's true," Della agreed. "You are very much alike."

"I'm proud to have her name," Julie said. "Some day I hope I will have the strength that she had inside herself."

"That's faith, Julie," Charles said quietly. "And you do have it. If you didn't, you would never have been able to capture your grandmother on canvas."

Julie looked at Charles, searching for understanding.

Dan started pulling the plastic down over the canvas.

"Oh, please, not yet!" Julie protested.

"Sorry, I've got to get back to the station and write the report on this whole episode." He made sure the plastic was secure and gently laid the painting back in its secure spot.

"It's almost worse to see it again and then have it taken away," Della said.

"This time it's only temporary, though," Larry said.

Julie choked back tears mixed with happiness and sorrow as she watched Dan Rakes back out of the driveway and head into town.

Still standing next to Larry, Julie turned to Charles. "I have a sketch you should see Charles," she said quietly.

"Is it what I think it is?"

She nodded.

"What's this about a sketch?" Larry asked suspiciously. "Have you two got a secret?"

Julie smiled and nodded. The time had come to tell Larry what was going on. "Actually, yes. Charles has been after me to paint something for the church."

"Oh? I didn't know that."

"I didn't mention it because I didn't think I could do it."

"And now you do?"

"I'm beginning to understand what it means to have faith. It's not at all what I always thought it would be like." She met Charles's gaze. "I'd like to try that painting, Charles. . . that is, if you like the sketch."

"If it comes from inside you, I'm sure I will. When can I see it."

"It's in the parlor. I left my pad on the couch."

"I'm on my way," Charles said, turning immediately to go into the house.

"I'll go with you," Della said. "We have something to celebrate. I'll get some goodies out."

Julie started to follow them, but Larry caught her arm. "Wait just a minute."

"What is it?"

"I know it's hard to see the painting go again, but I can see in your face how relieved you are to have it back."

"It's safe now."

"Before long, it will be back, hanging in Leed House just like we talked about."

Julie nodded silently, not sure of where Larry was leading the conversation.

"I want it to hang there for a long time," Larry said.

"It will," she assured him.

"I mean a very long time." He grasped her hand and squeezed it. "There's something I've been wanting to say ever since opening night. But with *Triumph* missing it just didn't seem like the right time."

She looked at him quizzically.

"This is not the right time, either," he continued, "but I have to get this out of my system." Larry reached into his shirt pocket and brought out a small box.

Julie's eyes widened. "Is that. . .is that what I think. . .?"

Larry laughed at her tongue-tied attempt to talk. "Yes, it's a ring, Julie. . .but not a diamond."

"Oh?" Now she was getting confused. What was going on?

He opened the box and held it out for her to see. A cluster of bright emeralds caught the sunlight and glinted in their gold setting. She leaned in to look at it closely.

"It's beautiful, Larry, but. . .?"

"This ring has been in our family a long time. In fact, it's one that my grandfather had when he was running his jewelry business."

"Your grandfather Lorenzo?"

"Right. Mom says he always kept this ring in a safe place. She only saw it once or twice while she was growing up, and he would never say why he kept it instead of selling it."

"It must have had some special meaning for him."

Larry nodded. "Now that we know about his relationship with your grandmother when they were younger, Mom and I have wondered if it was the ring that he had picked out for her."

Julie's eyes widened. "Do you think so?"

"We can only speculate. But that would explain why he always held on to it but wouldn't talk about it."

"It's lovely. Indescribable."

"I want you to wear it, Julie."

"But—"

"Of course, it's not a ring that we would ever let out of the family," Larry said. "So you'll also have to become a Paxton."

"So. . .this means. . .you want. . . ?"

"Yes, I want to marry you. Julie Covington, will you marry me?"

Julie choked back her surprise and answered confidently. "Yes, of course, I will."

Larry lifted the ring from its case and tenderly slid it onto her finger. Gently, Larry leaned down and kissed her.

epilogue

"I knew from the first moment I saw your sketch that I would like this painting." Dressed in a dark suit for a change, Pastor Charles Brooke leaned comfortably against the wall and studied the large canvas hanging in the foyer of the community church. In a few minutes, the congregation would gather around it and dedicate it to the glory of God.

A shiny, bluish hue pervaded the painting, which was full of movement and light, though the young woman at its center was standing still. Radiance from beyond the doorway had burst upon her, spotlighting her and raising her from the darker tones behind her. Despite the swirling chaos around her, her face was calm and confident.

Julie was pleased with what she had done.

"It's a truly beautiful piece of work, Julie. Thank you for putting yourself into it the way you did."

"Thank you for pushing me," Julie said. "If you hadn't, I might never have been able to express what little I understand about faith."

"I must admit, the title surprises me."

"Oh?"

"It was six months ago that I suggested you paint a *Faith Experiment*. Back then it was just a catchy phrase, something to challenge you. I never expected you to take it seriously as a title."

"I took the challenge seriously, so the title seemed appropriate."

"But why *Faith Experiment I*? That sounds like you are

planning a series."

"Faith is never finished," Julie explained. "I used to want to tie up the loose ends in my life into nice finished, secure knots that would never change, something that I could control and depend on. But there's no room for faith in that kind of life."

"So, perhaps there will be a series?" Charles said hopefully. "What will be your next experiment in faith?"

Julie threw her head back and laughed. "I'm getting married next week. I would say that qualifies as an experiment in faith."

"I heard that!" Larry's voice announced his presence. He set down a stack of hymnals on a small table. "Have I been reduced to the status of an experiment?"

Julie raised her face to receive his kiss. "Sorry, Sweetheart," she said. "You're not an experiment. But you have to admit that being married will be new territory. And there may be some dark days."

"The light will always shine through," Larry answered seriously, looking at the painting. "I promise you, you will always be able to see the light."

"Have you hung *Triumph* yet?" Charles asked.

Julie nodded eagerly. "Last night. Right over the fireplace in the main parlor."

"The perfect spot," Larry added.

"It's such a relief to have the trial over and actually have the paintings back," Julie said with a sigh of satisfaction. "Six months is a long time. *Triumph* is where it belongs now. I don't ever want to move it."

"Ah, so that's the real reason you agreed to marry me," Larry teased.

"Of course," Julie answered in the same tone. "Did you think there was another reason?"

Larry wrapped his arms around Julie and bent to kiss her. "Let me give you a few other reasons."

"That's enough, you two." Della had arrived. "Knock it off until next Saturday." She turned to look at the canvas. "This is such a beautiful painting. I just love the colors and the shading and the ambience it creates. It's perfect for the foyer, of course, and it will look absolutely wonderful hanging there for years and years to come. It will probably outlast the church."

Della stopped and looked from Charles to Larry to Julie. "I should stop talking, right?"

"Just slow down a bit, Mom," Larry said, smiling.

"I'm still worried that people will not understand it," Julie admitted.

"Why?" Charles asked.

"Because it's not religious enough. People will expect a picture from the Bible for hanging in a church."

"You painted something that comes from your life and your own encounter with faith. How could anything be more religious than that?" said Charles.

"Charles is right," Della said. "That painting speaks more than a year's worth of sermons."

"Hey!" Charles protested. "I'm not sure I like that."

Julie laughed. How grateful she was for these friends: Charles, with his acceptance of her questions and steady encouragement for her to find her own answers. Della, despite all her pampering and fussing, was someone Julie would trust with her life. And Larry. How lucky she was to have him promising to be at her side and walk toward the light with her. All three had played a role in the formation of *Faith Experiment I*. In the last two years, they had surrounded her, undergirded her, pushed and pulled from every direction because they believed in her more than she believed in herself.

A lump formed in her throat.

"Are the programs ready for the dedication service?" Charles asked, turning his attention to the reality of the moment.

"Yes, they were on the desk in the church office," Della said. "I'll get them."

People began to arrive and gather in the foyer. Julie smiled nervously as church members viewed the painting for the first time. Quizzical expressions dominated, although some faces showed understanding of her message. A few people murmured their appreciation for her talent and the gift to the church.

The crowd grew until it was time to begin. Equipped with hymnals and bulletins, the congregation followed Charles's instructions and gathered around the painting. Della insisted that Julie move to the front of the formation and stand with Charles next to the painting.

"Holy God, it is with gratitude that we come to You this morning," Charles intoned. "We celebrate the gift of creativity that You instill in us. We praise You for the emotions You stir in us. We honor You with our feeble expressions...of joy, of doubt, of gratitude, of despair, of faith."

Tears formed in Julie's eyes as she listened to Charles. She admired his ability to put into words what she could only put into a picture. He was not afraid to admit weakness. Neither was he afraid to seek strength in hidden places.

"Please join me for the responsive reading in your bulletin," Charles directed.

Julie fumbled for the paper, hardly able to focus on the words.

Charles began. "You are the Creator, and we praise You for the power to make something out of nothing."

And the people answered, "Glory to God, Who created the

earth and all the beauty therein."

"You are the Sustainer, and we praise You for the light of Your faithfulness in dark days."

"Glory to God, Who created the earth and all the beauty therein."

"You are the Savior, and we praise You for coming to earth to draw us to Yourself."

"Glory to God, Who created the earth and all the beauty therein."

"You are the Teacher, and we praise You for the lessons You teach us and the grace to learn them."

"Glory to God, Who created the earth and all the beauty therein."

Julie looked around the small crowd earnestly reading their responses at the appropriate times. Two years ago they had all been strangers, but they had welcomed her, doubts and all, into their midst. Today they celebrated with her the triumph of faith. Next week, they would witness her marriage to Larry Paxton.

Standing at the back of the group was Aunt Joanna, now ninety-seven years old, thin, and hunched more than ever. Though she looked as if a whisper would blow her over, her eyes were bright with pride. For a moment, Julie had a sense that her own grandmother was there in the room. She reached into her skirt pocket for a tissue.

"You are the Artist, and we praise You for the canvases of our lives, offering them to You for the brush strokes of Your mercy."

"Glory to God, Who created the earth and all the beauty therein."

"Please turn in your hymnals to number one-forty-eight." Charles started the hymn of praise with his clear bass voice.

As she groped to find the right page, Julie sensed motion

next to her. She looked up to see Larry offering to share his hymnal. She met his gaze and smiled, feeling instantly composed. Now she was able to lift her voice in song.

When the hymn finished, Charles went directly into a prayer. "Heavenly Father, we stand before You this morning as frail human beings, people who make mistakes, people with countless faults. But we offer ourselves to You. Let us be the canvas to which You touch Your brush. Let our lives bear the light of Your presence. We dedicate this painting to Your glory, with the prayer that it will be a constant reminder to each of us that You are the true light of the world. Amen."

And the refrain echoed in Julie's mind: *Glory to God, Who created the earth and all the beauty therein.*

A Letter To Our Readers

Dear Reader:

In order that we might better contribute to your reading enjoyment, we would appreciate your taking a few minutes to respond to the following questions. When completed, please return to the following:

Rebecca Germany, Editor
Heartsong Presents
P.O. Box 719
Uhrichsville, Ohio 44683

1. Did you enjoy reading *The Road Home*?
   ❏ Very much. I would like to see more books
     by this author!
   ❏ Moderately
     I would have enjoyed it more if _____

   _____

2. Are you a member of *Heartsong Presents*? Yes   No
   If no, where did you purchase this book? _____

   _____

3. What influenced your decision to purchase this
   book? (Check those that apply.)

   ❏ Cover   ❏ Back cover copy

   ❏ Title   ❏ Friends

   ❏ Publicity   ❏ Other _____

4. On a scale from 1 (poor) to 10 (superior), please rate the following elements.

    ___Heroine   ___Plot

    ___Hero   ___Inspirational theme

    ___Setting   ___Secondary characters

5. What settings would you like to see covered in *Heartsong Presents* books?

_____

_____

6. What are some inspirational themes you would like to see treated in future books?_____

_____

_____

7. Would you be interested in reading other *Heartsong Presents* titles?   ❏ Yes   ❏ No

8. Please check your age range:
❏ Under 18   ❏ 18-24   ❏ 25-34
❏ 35-45   ❏ 46-55   ❏ Over 55

9. How many hours per week do you read? ————

Name _____

Occupation _____

Address _____

City _____   State _____   Zip _____

Susannah Hayden

❀❀❀❀❀❀❀❀❀❀❀❀❀❀❀❀❀❀❀❀❀❀❀❀❀❀❀

__*A Matter of Choice*__—Stacie's new job promotion could mean the end of her future with Brad. . .or the start of a new and perhaps better life with Dillon. What life is Stacie to have? HP14

__*Between Love and Loyalty*__—Megan Browning and her friends are working frantically to keep the old Homestead Youth Camp running. Then Megan discovers that the young architect who has captured her heart is planning on developing Homestead into condominiums. HP69

_*The Road Before Me*__—Overwhelmed by self-doubt, Julie Covington searches for an answer. At her grandmother's childhood home in Maine she finds comfort and solace in the writings of a young girl, a girl who walked the same road as the one before Julie. HP77

__*Between the Memory and the Moment*__—Jenna seems happy living and working at the camp owned by Dillon Graves. After all, she's hopelessly in love with the much-older Dillon, and he genuinely appreciates her work. Still, Jenna feels compelled to move on. But to what? HP113

__*Farther Along the Road*__—Julie Covington wants to be accepted as a serious artist, and she wants to possess a love as vital as the one her grandmother had for her first love. When Larry Paxton displays interest in her paintings, Julie begins to feel hopeful that both needs can be fulfilled. HP117

·····Heart♥ng·····

Any 12
*Heartsong
Presents* titles
for only
$26.95 *

CONTEMPORARY ROMANCE IS CHEAPER BY THE DOZEN!

Buy any assortment of twelve *Heartsong Presents* titles and save 25% off of the already discounted price of $2.95 each!

*plus $1.00 shipping and handling per order and sales tax where applicable.

HEARTSONG PRESENTS TITLES AVAILABLE NOW:

·········· **Presents** ··········

*Temporarily out of stock.

Great Inspirational Romance at a Great Price!

Heartsong Presents books are inspirational romances in contemporary and historical settings, designed to give you an enjoyable, spirit-lifting reading experience. You can choose from 136 wonderfully written titles from some of today's best authors like Colleen L. Reece, Brenda Bancroft, Janelle Jamison, and many others.

When ordering quantities less than twelve, above titles are $2.95 each.

SEND TO: Heartsong Presents Reader's Service
P.O. Box 719, Uhrichsville, Ohio 44683

Please send me the items checked above. I am enclosing $_____
(please add $1.00 to cover postage per order. OH add 6.25% tax. NJ
add 6%.). Send check or money order, no cash or C.O.D.s, please.
To place a credit card order, call 1-800-847-8270.

NAME _____

ADDRESS _____

CITY/STATE_____ ZIP _____

HPS AUG.